Chance for Love

Chance for Love

ANN B. HARRISON

TULE
PUBLISHING

Dedication

My deepest gratitude to all the girls in the Tule team for helping bring this story to life. Lindsey, Danielle, Meghan, Sinclair and of course, Jane Porter.

Chapter One

T HE DOCTOR LOOKED at Chance, sympathy obvious in his eyes. "I'm sorry. You've done far more damage than even I can fix." He walked away from the lit up x-ray box where his patient's broken hip was on display and sat heavily in his chair, swinging it around to look at Chance. "You should get more movement in your leg once the hip heals better, but I'm afraid there will be no more bull riding for you."

Chance Watson swallowed the bile rising in his throat. The quick rush of emotions threatened to tip him over the edge if he didn't get a grip on them. He'd been expecting something like this, but it still rocked his world. His first big injury was also going to be his last. How ironic was that?

He cleared his throat before he spoke. "It's all I know. Not sure how I'm going to go back to running a ranch without the thrill of upcoming competitions to look forward to."

"Well now, I'm sure once you get used to it, you'll manage just fine. Your granddaddy bred some of the best bucking bulls in Montana back in his day, before he passed on and left it all to you. Don't see why you can't take over the reins now it's time." The doctor leaned back in his chair. "You know, he'd be right proud of what you've achieved in your career. Champion bull rider for what, twelve years in a row? Can't say I know of anyone else who's had as long a career on the IBR tour as you have."

Chance snorted and looked away. He'd had an amazing career and as far as he was concerned, it was still flourishing. Or at least it had been until his injury this season. "How much longer until you can take the pins out of my hip?"

The doctor leaned forward and reached for his laptop, flicking through the dates. "I can take you into surgery in five weeks. I don't see any reason why the bones wouldn't have knitted well enough by then so long as you don't take any knocks to the bone. Pretty standard procedure so you'd only be in overnight." He turned from the screen and smiled. "Go home to Marietta, Chance, and rest up. You have the ranch to fall back on and I'm sure with a little bit of help you'll do well. Just that you'll be on the other side of the bulls from now on. Breeding them, not riding them. Much safer in my opinion. Last thing I wanted was to see you here in this state."

Chance stood up with the help of his cane, getting his balance before letting go of the edge of the chair. He tried to stand tall but the pain in his hip made it almost impossible for him to stretch out to his full height of six feet three inches.

"My nurse will be in touch the week before the operation to go over the arrangements for admission. Go and start your new life. Kick back and think of doing something that won't give your body such a hard time from now on. You've earned the retirement and looking at all the bruises and scars you're carrying, it's not before time either."

"Sure, Doc. Ranching fulltime sounds just like the ticket to me right now." He couldn't keep the bitterness from his voice, but deep down he wondered if this was what he was looking for.

The tour had lost its appeal over the last couple of years and he'd been having trouble trying to figure out why. The drinking, women, and parties no longer appealed, nor did being in the public eye give him the thrill it used to. The modeling shoots for his sponsors used to make him feel proud, cocky even. Lately he'd felt out of sorts, strutting around in the latest clothes, boots, and sunglasses for ad campaigns that would see his pictures all over billboards and magazines. The only thing that had made him feel satisfied was his own line of products and seeing them hit the shelves.

"You have younger brothers, don't you? Surely one of them can help you out until you're on your feet."

"I'll be fine, Doc. Always someone wanting to work for me. See you later and thanks."

Chance put his hat on his head before he shook the doctor's hand and headed out of his office. At the curb, Ralph,

Chance's old school friend and fellow competitor, sat on the hood of his car.

"Ouch, looks like someone got bad news." Ralph stood when Chance hobbled toward him and he hurried to open the back door, holding his hand out to help his best friend.

Once Chance was settled inside, he dropped the cane to the floor. *Raising bulls instead of riding them isn't exactly what I'd planned on this year. My career can't be over, not just yet. Not when I'm still the toast of Montana and the IBR tour.* But perhaps it was what he'd been looking for, why he'd felt so unsettled, and why Terror – two tons of bucking fury – had gotten the better of him. Sometimes things happened for the best reasons even if it didn't feel like it at the time.

"Where to, Chance? Back to the hotel?" Ralph grinned at him from over his shoulder, waiting for instructions.

"Yeah, but we won't be staying there for long. I'm expected at the office for a catch-up with the boys from the International Bull Riders to fill them in on future plans. While I'm there, I need you to grab my bags and then you can drop me at the airport if you don't mind. I'm heading home to the ranch. I have things to sort out."

CALLIE LISTER GAZED out at the red, barren land just outside of Alice Springs in the Northern Territory, Australia. This place was her home, always had been, and she'd expected to grow old here, just like her father's parents and his parents before that. Her father regaled her with tales of how she would take over when he was too old to work, letting her run the station as she saw fit. She would make sure her sisters could work alongside her as well, if that was what they chose to do, still keeping the spread in the family for future generations.

But now that was all gone...or would be by the end of the week. The accident that took both of her parents brought home the cruel reality of life in the outback. All in the form of a letter from the bank delivered just days after the funeral that saw both of her parents buried under the unforgiving, red earth because a tired driver caused them both to be taken far too young.

"Callie." The youngest of the twins, Jess, stood at the gate of the house paddock, looking unsure of whether to approach her or not. Tears streaked down her thin pale face and Callie held open her arms to her sister. Together they stood in the dusty, barren yard, holding each other up against the onslaught of pain threatening to knock them down.

"Hush. It will alright, you'll see." Callie brushed the damp hair from Jess's face. At three weeks shy of sixteen, Jess was the more sensitive of the twins. She was the one who always felt the pain or disappointment in life whereas her sister Lori was pragmatic and down to earth. It was she who was packing the twins' belongings to move to the city to live with their father's parents so they could attend university and get a better education.

"I don't want to go. I want to stay with you."

Callie pushed her back and wiped her thumbs under Jess's eyes to stay the tears. "You can't and we both know it. I have to do this; I have no other choice if we want the family name to not be tarnished with debt. I won't let Mum and Dad have their names run through the mud this way. You've heard what's happening in town already. They don't need to be the gossip at the local pub because they died leaving us to sort out the bank. I won't do that to them."

"But you'll leave us alone." She hiccupped and the tears trickled down, making twin paths across her freckled cheeks.

"You won't be alone. You have Grandpa and Nana and I'll be home as soon as my contract ends. I don't have a choice and you know it."

"Get a job here on another station. There must be someone who will employ you."

"There isn't. Besides, the money isn't that good here anymore, not with the drought hitting everyone as hard as it has. Plus, I don't know anything else but farming. I wouldn't stand a hope in hell of getting a job in the city either, Jess. I'm better off taking this chance and going to America. The rancher is offering great money for a twelve-month contract with all the perks and a bonus at the end of it if I manage to up the stock numbers." She stroked her sister's hair, willing her to understand. "I need that bonus. The banks told us in no uncertain terms what our position is. It's not fair but we can't change it. I will not let our parents be remembered for leaving us rolling in debt. They deserve more than that. Maybe then I can come back and we can start again, maybe find a new place if the bank has sold our home off."

Callie was holding onto the hope that with so many farmers walking off their properties due to crippling debt and high interest rates, their little slice of heaven would still be sitting here when her contract ran out in America. But would she be able to come back with enough money to buy it or would she be happy to clear her parents name and move on?

If the twins made the move from country to city and adjusted well enough, she could take the time to make her own life so long as their schooling was covered. Financially, she was responsible for them and their needs came before hers.

I don't know if I can get away after the time limit is up. Twelve months will go fast, especially if I work hard and save my money but will it be long enough?

"But…"

"No buts. Stay strong and go and help Lori pack your stuff. Grandpa will be here soon and I doubt he will want to hang around much. It's a long drive to town." She watched Jess slowly make her way back inside the house, shoulders hunched over in defeat.

Callie looked at the weatherboard home. The peeling paint, rickety fences, and broken concrete path up to uneven front steps. No matter how bad it looked to the casual observer, it was the only home she'd ever known and she'd miss it terribly. She closed her eyes, opened them again, and focused on it, knowing she could only take her memories with her when she left.

The bank had been quite clear on that. Nothing was to be removed apart from their personal effects. No machinery or stock was to be touched. Anything of value would be sold off to put against the debt. Not that they had much anyway. Life was too tough for extras and that had never been a problem for any of them. They were happy living on the station, working the land as they had. There weren't many trips into Alice Springs apart from the drive for supplies once a month. It was then that Callie got excited. They picked up the lessons from the post office for home schooling when they were younger, and her favorite treat of all was the magazines they were allowed.

While the twins had been into fashion magazines, Callie's favorite had been the *Horse and Cattle Digest*. She would climb up on the hay bales in the barn and lose herself between the pages for hours. After she'd read every single word, she would take her ever-suffering, old quarter horse and put him through the paces as if she was in the rodeo and he was a stud-worthy, blue-ribbon winner. Her mother, an American by birth, had told Callie bedtime stories of the rodeo and encouraged her to dream big, hoping that one day her daughter would get her own chance at the rodeo she so craved.

As she'd grown older and more realistic, she'd dreamed that one day the farm could afford to buy stock like those between the pages of the glossy magazine. Sadly it was not to be, and the reality had hit hard when the local police had come to inform the girls of the accident that had taken both parents from them.

Callie's things were already packed and sitting on the end of her bed ready to go. Her work visa and passport were tucked in the side of the old canvas carryall bag along with a photo of her parents and the three girls sitting together on the old, rickety veranda. She was leaning on her father's shoulder, her arms draped over his chest and he was holding her hands, laughing up into her face. Her sisters were both perched on their mother's lap, faces close together and hands linked. Callie couldn't remember who had taken the photograph, but it was the only one of them all together in recent years.

The sound of a car traveling over the cattle grid by the roadway caught her attention. Her grandfather was here. She watched as he drove down the drive, doing his best to avoid the large pot holes that jarred even her teeth. She winced as he hit a particularly big one and the bumper made contact with the red rock of the driveway.

"Callie." Jock Lister pulled up beside her and opened the car door, got out, and stood in front of her. He held out his arms and she fell against him, giving into one last bout of tears before she said goodbye to everything she knew and loved. He patted her back as she cried and pulled out a handkerchief when she moved away from him.

"Thanks, Grandpa. I didn't mean to cry all over you."

"Honey, I don't care. I just wish your grandmother and I could do more for you. We both want you to come back and stay with us in the city, you know that. There's no reason to go flying off to another country to make a decent living. You can do that right here in Australia."

"No, I can't. I'm not qualified to do anything other than run a station, as much as we might like to think differently. I'll be okay, I promise. I'm twenty-six years old for goodness sakes. Probably time I left home anyway. I might even be able to catch up with some of Mum's family while I'm over there."

"That would make this old man feel better. At least you have a job to go to anyway. Better than rocking up with nothing planned."

Oh, Grandpa, if only you knew what I have planned. You'd hog tie me to a fence and not let me go. But I have no other choice if I want to clear the debts on this place and make a future for my sisters.

How could she tell him she knew they would struggle on their pension to bring up two teenagers let alone have the money for them to go to university? His pride would be damaged beyond repair. Losing his only son and his wife had been bad enough, finding out the debt they left behind had forced her to sign up to marry a stranger because she felt backed into a corner with no choice would kill him. She wouldn't do that to her grandfather.

Her sisters were relying on him to keep them safe while Callie tried to bring home the money that would keep them out of the poorhouse and lift their parent's reputation out of the dust. And she was relying on the wages she brought in to make a nest egg for the girls. They'd get enough education to enable them to qualify for a decent job.

Chapter Two

"YOU'VE GOT TO be fucking kidding me. I don't see why you can't hire on Jethro. He's been asking you for a job for ages. And I'm sure there're plenty of guys local who'd love to work here for the great Chance Watson." Tyson followed his older brother up the stairs and slowed his steps to match Chance's battle with his cane.

"It doesn't concern you, understand?" Chance hobbled to and fro in the walk in wardrobe, riffling through his clothes rack, looking for something suitable for his upcoming Las Vegas wedding. He chose a plain black jacket and trousers, a black shirt, and walked out to throw them on the bed. Then he went back and chose a pair of boots and a thin tie to match. All black like doom and gloom. Perhaps he should change the tie, try for a slightly more cheerful theme?

"It does. He needs the job and you need him."

Chance turned on Tyson. "I refuse to leave my ranch in the hands of that cowboy. Have you even seen what he's done to his grandfather's place?"

Tyson looked down at his foot, tapped the floor with his

boot.

"Yeah, you have. That old man is desperate for help on the ranch and what do his grandsons do? Nothing apart from drink and get into bar fights in town. Silly, old fool should have given them their marching orders years ago. Last time I saw, the stock was poorly, the pastures a mess of tumbleweeds and scrub, and fences down all over the place. If you think I'm leaving my ranch, the one that our grandfather built from scratch, to a lazy, beer guzzling, immature—"

Tyson held up his hands. "Okay, okay."

"So now you know why I've employed my own kind of worker. I don't want to hear anymore about it."

"You're only doing this so we don't have to help you out. For crying out loud, Chance, we're all brothers. We help each other, that's how families work."

Chance turned around, a red necktie in his hand, and stared at Tyson. He was prepared for the attitude about bringing in a new manager but not the passion his younger brother was showing or the negativity that fairly oozed from his skin. "You all have your own lives, and you have your own ranch. I need help and I'm sick and tired of leaving my place in the hands of someone who claims to know what they're doing because they spent a summer on a dude ranch and doesn't have a freaking clue how life really works out here. It's time I hired someone who knows the job and if I have to import them from overseas, so be it."

"What, so you're bringing someone from Australia to

run it for you? I don't believe you can't hire somebody local. Not all are useless out here." Tyson ran his hand through his thick, black hair and cursed again. "You know I don't mind keeping an eye on things. Just can't be here every day, but now you're back home, you should be able to get by with just a couple of hands."

"And that's what I'm getting at. I've tried to bring in people to run the place that claim to know what they're doing. A couple of hands hasn't worked in the past, but this person knows the way of life and has the experience to back that up. I figure it's a safer bet. Besides, nobody apart from your friend applied. Believe me, I'm disappointed too but there you have it."

Tyson dropped down onto the super king-sized bed and watched Chance pack an overnight bag. "What are you doing? Thought you said you were picking them up from the airport. Not like you to dress up all fancy like unless you were expecting to get laid while you were there. Doing a little something on the side, brother?"

"Mind your own business, Tyson. Now scat. Go on home to your horses and your own life. I'm fine, everything is under control." He zipped up the suit bag and threw a package of toiletries into the small suitcase.

Tyson stood up. "Fine then. Be like that. Just wait until the boys in town hear you've gone and brought in a foreigner to run the place instead of giving the job to Jethro when you go back to the tour. They're not going to like it at all. You know how we like to keep things in the family."

I'm not going back, ever. "Well that's just too damned bad, they had their chance to apply, and feel free to tell them why I didn't employ Jethro, too, or I will. And I don't want you wasting all your time up here when you have your own place and more than enough to do. The other boys are living away so I can't rely on them, nor should I have to."

"You know Rory lost his grip on reality when his wife died. He needed to get away or he would have gone crazy with everything the same and her gone. You can't blame him."

"Yeah, well, that's his call. This here is mine." Chance pushed Tyson out the door and hooked the bags over his shoulder while using his cane to steady his leg.

The brothers headed down the sweeping staircase of the huge log home Chance had built six years ago not long after their grandfather died and left him the property. His meteoritic rise to fame on the IBR tour and his wise investments had given him more cash than he could spend on a good day, but this was his dream for the time when he was too old to ride bulls. All part of his plan and the reason he'd set up his business the way he had. He just hadn't expected it to come around quite so soon or in such a painful way.

The home was set against the backdrop of the Rocky Mountains with views from the front rooms of the house over Copper Mountain and down into the town. The two story building looked like it jutted out of the wooded hills with acres and acres of rich green pastures spread out all around it. But once one drove up the long, winding driveway and got closer to the house, they could see the pine forests were set well back at the base of the mountains which were already tipped with a fine dusting of snow.

He threw his case in the bed of the big, black truck and hung the suit bag in the back of the cab. "Don't worry about me, I'll be fine and so will the new ranch manager. Trust me when I say I have it all under control."

Tyson shook his head before he looked up into Chance's face. "If'n you say so then. Let me know when you get back home. I want to see this guy and make sure he knows what he's doing before you go back on the tour. Would hate to get any surprises while you're away winning more hearts and making dollars."

"Sure."

"Talking of which, are you going to marry that actress I saw you with on the television entertainment show? You know the one with the Barbie figure and jet black hair— Libby Tucker?"

"Not telling you any of my secrets. Now get on outta here. I have things to do, places to go." Chance hooked his arm over his brother's shoulder and gave him a quick man hug before pushing him toward his own truck. He watched Tyson jump into the cab and start the engine. Chance remained standing there long after the rumble of the truck could no longer be heard on its trip down the mountain.

The sun shone down on his face and he took the time to look around the hill at the ranch he had built up in the off seasons. His big log home shadowed the tiny cabin his grandfather had lived in. The young bulls were grazing in the paddocks, oblivious to the turmoil racing through his mind. He'd wanted to tell his brother about Callie, the girl from Australia, but he didn't know how Tyson would react and if he'd go blabbing to the other boys. Last thing Chance needed was them all descending on the ranch while he was still trying to get to know his new wife. Not that it was any of their business, but the brothers were close, always had been. Especially after their mother had died young and the old man had taken to a bottle to drown his sorrows.

Chance had run away to the rodeo to deal with the pain. Luckily he was damned good at it, especially the bull riding where the top money was. It'd been fun at first, riding and winning to the cheer of the crowds. Going from town to town, winning the small points before he could take on the big guns at the IBR where the money was better. Eventually he'd made a name for himself and he'd been hooked into the lifestyle faster than a bull out of a chute.

Parties and television appearances had become second nature and for awhile he'd loved the attention and the adrenaline rush of it all. Things had eventually started to wear thin where late nights were concerned and his body felt tired and ached more than he wanted it to. Maybe that was why he'd lost concentration on his last bull ride.

Guilt at leaving his brothers at home with their father tugged at Chance over the years and he always made sure they were doing okay. His grandfather had kept an eye on them, too, but that hadn't eased Chance's guilt at running away leaving them behind. Chance earned good money on the tour, and it had been easy to transfer lump sums into his brother's accounts via his grandfather, which in turn made him feel less guilty about his increasing wealth and leaving them behind.

His high profile and his business dealings identified him as a magnet for those who wanted to brush sides with the rich and famous, and he was never without either a model or a starlet on his arm. Libby Tucker was the latest in a long line of beauties who professed true love. They made the tabloids on a regular basis and of course Tyson would have seen them together. Stood to reason he'd think Chance was due to get hitched sooner or later. But she'd already shown her true colors, and Chance couldn't bear the thought of being hurt again.

Being young and inexperienced in the ways of the world had been his excuse for falling in love, being used and then dumped when he was first making headlines and winning rodeos. Now it would sound pathetic to hear a man looking for true love had been duped by a wannabe famous actress and left picking up his broken heart when her attention moved to the next rising star. When he told them of his dream of living out his life on the ranch it wasn't the same as what they wanted to hear and they couldn't get away fast enough.

In the early years, he'd been quick to fall in love, desperate he'd come to understand, to make up for the love he'd been missing since his mother died. His father was already a difficult man and after Chance's mother had passed away, his childhood had gone downhill. Bouts of heavy drinking, violent behavior colored his early years.

He turned and gazed at the top paddock closest to the barn behind the house. The big grey bull, Terror, stood beside the fence as if he knew what was going through Chance's mind. The same beast that had thrown him into the fence at the last championship, causing him a career ending injury, chewed his grass and ignored the man standing before him. He'd pawed at Chance while he lay unconscious on the ground keeping everyone away from him while he lay bleeding. Now he was standing looking as docile as a milking cow. But Chance knew better. He knew the sudden turn of attitude that could run through this bull at the snap of a finger for no good reason. The bull was naturally cantankerous and his moods hard to read at the best of times.

He was a formidable animal, solid muscle, built like a tank, and very fast for his size. That was what made him the perfect breeder for the rodeo bulls Chance planned to specialize in. "You'd better pay well for what you did to me, you cantankerous old bastard. When I get home, you're going out to stud again. Let's see if you can do better than last year. Make sure you know what you're doing and do it well, or you'll end up on the barbeque."

Chance turned and opened the door to his truck and climbed in, throwing the cane on the seat beside him. He started the ignition and cruised down the driveway to go and meet his wife-to-be in Las Vegas where he had already planned the wedding.

CALLIE LOOKED AROUND the room. The bellhop stood at the door and coughed to clear his throat or get her attention. She looked at him, confused and tired. "I'm sorry. Did I forget something?" She looked at her bag where he had left it on the end of the bed before the penny dropped. His tip.

Shame rushed up her cheeks. She'd been so nervous the whole flight over, she'd completely forgotten about the local customs she read about in the traveler's guide book she'd picked up at the airport before leaving Australia. Precious money she couldn't afford to spend at the time, now almost wasted because she'd forgotten almost everything she'd read. Nerves were getting the better of her.

"Sorry. Not thinking." She hurried to grab her purse from the hippie bag on the small dining table and looked at the small amount of American change she had left over from the taxi ride. Until her new "husband" arrived, it was all the money she had left in the world. Every cent he'd already given her had gone straight to the bank.

Callie apologized again as she handed over the coins, her stomach sinking as she dropped them into his palm. "I have to change some more money before I go shopping. Sorry."

"Thank you, ma'am, that is very kind of you." He gripped the coins in his hand and turned to walk out of the room. The door shut quietly behind him, leaving her alone in a strange hotel on the other side of the world wondering, once again, if there could have been another option out of their predicament.

What the hell possessed me to think this would work? Callie walked over to the window and looked down on the famous Las Vegas strip. It was just after sunset and the lights of the casinos and the local attractions lit up the main street now packed with tourists. She wasn't used to seeing so many people in one place, roaming, having a good time. Cars cruised up the road, tooting out greetings and ducking in and out of hotel driveways. She'd never seen so many stretch limos before nor had she seen so many colorful characters.

When she had walked into the hotel to check in earlier, she'd been assaulted by the noise of the casino and its gambling machines in the lobby. Blown away by the people around her looking as though they were all in party mode, she'd stumbled into a couple of scantily clad ladies, spilling the champagne from one of their glasses onto the tiled floor. They were both hanging onto the arm of a slightly inebriated man dressed like a cowboy. He was wearing tight denim jeans, a checkered shirt, and a large Stetson, jammed jauntily on his head. But it was his intricately worked boots that Callie noticed most of all.

"Hey, watch yourself." One of the women pushed her out of the way and she stumbled backwards and fell to the ground, landing ungracefully on her butt. Her eyes filled with tears of exhaustion and embarrassment. The carved boots she had spied a moment ago which had in all likeli-hood hood distracted her more than anything, appeared in her line of vision.

Callie looked up. The man held out a hand to her and waited with a grin on his face for her to take his offer. Resting her hand in his, she let him pull her to her feet.

"Best you watch where you're going, little lady."

"Sorry, I was kind of amazed at all the goings on here. It's not what I expected." She stared as a native Indian in full dress waltzed past her, shooting fire from his mouth with the help of a flaming torch.

"Does kind of blow you away now, don't it?" He gripped her hand tighter and she took a step back. "Now that's not right friendly of you, darlin'."

"Let me go, please." She wrenched her hand free, gripped her bag firmly, and turned away toward the desk. The laughter from the cowboy and his lady friends followed her as she stood in line to check-in, now wary of all the strangers milling around her.

When it was her turn to step up to the desk, Callie gave her name, hoping she wasn't going to be told there was nothing for her. She was still unsure if this crazy jaunt was going to amount to anything or if she would be left with no money and no place to go. The feeling of impending doom had stuck with her all the way over on her flight and ramped up now waiting to see if she had a room. To come all of this way on the man's word alone was irresponsible and stupid, but it was a last ditch attempt to make some decent money and pay off the family's debts.

"Yes, here we are, Miss Callie Lister, the Lido Suite." The receptionist clicked a few keys and smiled at her. "Your passport please, Miss Lister."

Callie handed it over and watched as it was checked before being handed back. The smiling woman tapped a bell beside her computer and a bellhop hurried over to take her bag. "Leo will show you to your suite, Miss Lister. Please call down for dinner when you're ready, I have it booked for seven thirty but feel free to change it. A butler is waiting by to serve you this evening as Mr. Watson felt you would be exhausted from your flight and would probably like an early night. Your car is booked for ten am tomorrow morning. Breakfast is available twenty-four hours, but might I suggest you eat by eight am to make your appointment?" She smiled at Callie and handed the key to the bellhop. "Enjoy your stay with us, Miss Lister."

The click of the door closing behind him brought her

back to the present. She bit her lip. Never before had she stayed in a hotel and she never imagined she would ever in all of her life stay in something as flashy as this. It was like a palace, something she'd only ever seen on a television program. The lounge dining room she was standing in was almost bigger than the house she grew up in. A small, white baby grand piano took pride of place over by a set of French doors with gold edged drapes pooling on the floor like a wave of melted bullion.

A marble fireplace was set into one wall with a large portrait of a young Edwardian girl standing with a small dog at her feet hanging above. Callie shook her head. It seemed so out of place in this desert town but, after the drive in from the airport, she doubted she could be surprised by anything else she saw. Double doors were slightly ajar and she walked over, taking a peek into the room beyond. A giant bed sat in the middle of the room, facing yet another set of French doors that opened onto a small Juliet-type balcony.

She walked in, trailed her hand over the bed before pushing down on the cover. The mattress moved under her fingers, dipping down like a cloud and she longed to climb under the covers now, forgoing dinner. Her stomach rumbled in protest and the toot of a car horn distracted her.

Callie walked over and pulled open the door, stepping outside to take a sniff of the night air and watch the tourists milling out along the pavement. The sounds rolled over her body, the noise of it all making her wince. For a short time as they'd dropped down over the red hills of Nevada, she'd had the feeling she could be home in Alice Springs but that thought was quickly pushed to one side as soon as she stepped off the plane. Standing outside on the balcony only brought it all back. She was as far from home as she could imagine and the people she had met so far were nothing like she was used to. Flamboyant and loud, the surroundings gave her a headache. She stepped back inside and shut the door on the outside world.

Callie explored the rest of her suite and discovered a bathroom to end all bathrooms. A deep tub was set in a marble surround, half sunken into the floor with an impressive array of buttons on one side. A tray on the edge of the bath held a selection of pretty bottles and she crouched down, leaned over and picked one up. When she unscrewed the top, a soft and fruity perfume reached her nostrils and she breathed it in deeply.

Before she could change her mind, she popped in the plug and turned on the taps. Callie poured the contents of the small bottle under the flow of water and watched the suds build up, covering the surface like fluffy clouds. She checked that the door was shut in the lounge before shucking off her dusty, worn, leather work boots and threw them on the floor beside the bed. As she walked back into the bathroom, Callie undid the buttons on her shirt, peeled it off her shoulders, and let it fall to the tiled floor. Her faded denim jeans quickly followed along with her panties and bra.

She turned the light down to a soft glow before dipping her toes into the fragrant water filling the huge tub. With a sigh of pleasure, Callie folded her travel weary body into the suds and leaned back, resting her toes on the tap to give it a gentle push when the water reached just over the tips of her nipples.

The buttons on the side of the tub were explored one by one and when a soft rhythm of water pulsed around her body, she closed her eyes. The only sound was the flow of the water running through the jets in the tub which shut out all of the rush and bustle of the outside world.

The soft tap on the door and a discreet cough woke her up. She squealed and covered her breasts.

"Sorry, ma'am, but dinner is almost ready to be served. Can I say around five minutes?"

"Um, ah, sure. Just let me get dressed please and I'll come out." She cast her gaze frantically around the room for something to cover up with.

"I do believe there is a fluffy robe behind the bathroom door, ma'am. Perhaps you would be happier dressed in that tonight since you won't be leaving the suite."

"Um, sure. If you think that's alright." She pulled the plug and sat in the cool water, watching it flow down the drain.

"Entirely up to you, ma'am." He cleared his throat and she heard the soft footsteps move away from the door.

Callie stood up and reached for a warm towel from the

heated towel rack beside the bath. She draped it around herself enjoying the warmth after the cool water. How long had she been in there? The time difference was messing with her head and she had no idea what time was anymore. It would probably take her a few days to get used to the new time zone and the best way to do that was to sleep through it, in her opinion.

There was indeed a fluffy white dressing gown behind the door. Thick and soft, it was the thing dreams were made of. Never before had she ever dressed in something this nice and luxurious. Her old dressing gown at home had seen better days but she'd refused to part with the pale blue chenille hand-me-down, wearing it like a second skin after her shower at night until faced with the inevitable wardrobe culling prior to her move. She wrapped the thick cover around herself, groaning in pleasure as the fabric brushed against her skin. The marble flooring was cool on her bare feet and she slid on a pair of matching slippers, digging her toes into the soft clouds of comfort.

The muffled sounds of someone working came from the lounge and she took a quick look in the mirror before venturing out. Callie looked tired and there was no getting away from that. Her body sagged from exhaustion and it was tempting to climb into the huge, comfy bed in the other room. She'd even forgo dinner for the extra half an hour's sleep she would probably get.

"How lovely to meet you, Miss Lister. My name is Bronson." The elderly gentleman was dressed in a black suit and looked very classy as he set her place at the table. "I usually butler for Mr. Chance whenever he's in town and it's my pleasure to serve you while you're here. I took the liberty of ordering you a meal tonight as I knew you would probably be tired and slightly thrown out by the time zone. Mr. Chance usually likes his steak so I ordered you his favorite dish."

Callie smiled and walked toward the table. It was set for one with a heated serving tray waiting beside it. She took the chair Bronson held out and sat down. The smell reached her nostrils, making her stomach sit up and take notice before he even pushed her chair in. She held her hand over her belly as it rumbled.

"I'm sorry. I didn't realize I was so hungry."

"At least we know the meal will be appreciated, ma'am."

Bronson placed a napkin on her lap before he took the lid from the hot plate. He served her a medium rare steak with asparagus and baby potatoes dripping in a butter sauce. When Callie picked up her knife, Bronson held up a bottle of champagne toward her glass.

"Uh, no thanks. I don't usually drink much."

He smiled at her. "Might I suggest a small glass just to help you sleep tonight? You have had an eventful day and I'm sure you want to be looking your best tomorrow when you meet Mr. Chance."

Callie blushed, wondering how much the butler knew.

"Thanks." She watched him pour the golden liquid, mesmerized by the bubbles rising in the crystal glass. Once the glass was full, the butler left her alone to eat her meal in peace. She heard him wandering around in the bedroom and bathroom and dreaded what he might be doing. Cleaning up her mess was her job, always had been. She'd left her clothes strewn all over the floor and now felt ashamed of her laziness. Oh well, next time she would be a little bit more careful.

The meat was tender and moist, just how she liked it, but this was steak like she'd never had before. It was juicy and succulent, with a smoky tang that lingered on her tongue and left her hungry for more. The flavors woke her up and she surprised herself by polishing off the whole meal. She made sure to sip at her wine, too, lest Branson chide her. The bubbles raced over her tongue and sparked an interest. She glanced at the bottle in the bucket of ice and couldn't read a word the label said. Something foreign and strange. She could get used to this kind of treatment, including the wine.

"Did you enjoy your meal, ma'am?"

Callie jumped. She hadn't heard him return to the lounge. "Yes, it was perfect. Thank you very much."

He cleared her plate and cutlery before setting another small plate in front of her. A single serve cheesecake with fresh raspberries bound in a nest of chocolate sat tempting her taste buds. "I really don't think—"

"Enjoy, ma'am. Mr. Chance insisted I feed you adequately. He dislikes women who try to survive on lettuce leaves or less." He sniffed delicately. "Not that you look like the lettuce leaf type of person, ma'am, if you don't mind me saying so."

She picked up the spoon and dipped into the cheesecake, taking a moment to savor the carefully created artwork. It seemed a shame to destroy what someone had taken the care to produce but, once tempted, there was no going back. Once the dessert hit her tongue, she groaned in pleasure. The taste of white chocolate underlined with a hint of fruit melted in her mouth.

Brandon smiled and nodded his head in approval. "Another of Mr. Chance's favorites."

"I'm understanding why, too." Callie licked the spoon clean before dipping it in the remaining desert.

"For breakfast tomorrow, I thought an omelet with cheese and herbs, and whole grain toast with honey. Perhaps a pot of tea. Is that acceptable for you?"

"You really don't have to go to any fuss. I'm happy with just toast."

"Ah, but you have a lot happening tomorrow. After your appointment with Mr. Chance, you have a long drive ahead of you back to the ranch. I wouldn't want you to attempt either thing without a decent breakfast." He smiled in a grandfatherly way. "I'm a firm believer that you can face anything the world throws at you if you have a decent breakfast."

She put down her spoon and looked at the butler, heat creeping up her cheeks. "You know what's happening tomorrow, don't you?"

"I must admit I'm privy to Mr. Chance's movements, yes. I had the pleasure of arranging the car and the venue for your nuptials." He folded his hands behind his back and looked at her.

"Must seem strange to you, me coming all this way to marry a man I don't even know."

"Well, now, far be it from me to make assumptions, ma'am. Mr. Chance does what he pleases and nobody would dare to question him why, least of all me, but I do suspect he knows what he is doing. I'm sure you're just what he needs, too, at this time in his life." He leaned forward, cleared away her plate, and tidied the table while Callie sat there watching. She toyed with the stem of her glass and finally finished the champagne before handing it to the butler.

"Well, guess I'd better get my beauty sleep then. Can't show up for my wedding looking like I just dragged myself in from the back paddocks."

"I unpacked your bag, ma'am, and didn't notice a dress for the occasion. Mr. Chance gave me permission to rectify that if I thought I needed to. I'll have something sent up first thing in the morning. Sleep well, Miss Callie." He smiled and took the trolley, pushing it from the room.

Holy heck, she'd forgotten to buy a dress. How could she

even think of rocking up to her wedding with nothing other than jeans and work shirts? It had been on her to do list but her bus had arrived in the city late and she didn't have enough time before she caught her flight from Australia. Then it had simply slipped her mind.

Chapter Three

C HANCE STOOD INSIDE the office at the wedding chapel door, watching the hovering paparazzi who normally staked out these venues in the hope of scooping a story for whatever sleazy tabloid would buy them. The Elvis Presley Chapel was always busy and there was the chance someone famous could sneak into Vegas for that quick behind the scenes wedding they seemed to love. The last thing he wanted was to be recognized. Not that it would cause a stir as much as an actor being here would, but he wanted to be the one who told his family he was married and that would be on his time schedule, not a trashy magazine's.

It might have been a tacky place to tie the knot, but he thought the humor of it might help break the ice for Callie. His nerves were pulled tight so he could imagine what she was feeling right now after flying halfway across the world to marry someone she'd never met before; after all she'd been through.

He looked at his watch. 10:05. She was already late and that would have been acceptable for the normal bride, but this was nothing like a normal wedding and he hoped she hadn't changed her mind. It was a contract pure and simple. The last thing he needed was for anyone to catch on to what he was doing until he was already safe and sound at home with his new wife away from prying eyes.

When he announced his divorce in twelve months' time and swore off marriage for life, he hoped he'd no longer be seen as marriageable material. Someone else would hold the top spot at the rodeo and be more appealing to those looking for a husband with fame and fortune while he got to live his life in peace and quiet.

An involuntary sigh of relief escaped his lips as he watched the black limo pull into the driveway. The driver jumped out and hurried to open the door for his bride-to-be. Chance stood back from the window as the paparazzi hurried forward, realized it wasn't anyone they knew and then back away again. He would wait for her to come inside before he made his presence known.

Not being dramatic, just careful because he had the feeling she wouldn't appreciate a spectacle either. Nor would his sponsors, considering he hadn't informed them yet of his retirement. He knew they would want to protect his brand as much as he did. Over the years he'd put a lot of time and effort into the products he'd put his name to and wanted that to continue.

From the brief Skype meeting with Callie, he'd decided she was a quiet, private sort of person with her own reasons for taking this step over and above the ones she'd shared with him and seeing herself splashed over the pages of the latest magazines wouldn't appeal to her. The world wasn't going to find out what he was doing until it was well over and done with.

There was a tap at the door and the Elvis minister popped his head through the open area. "Ready when you are."

Chance wiped his suddenly sweaty palms on his black trousers and swallowed down a sudden spurt of panic. *Here goes nothing.* He breathed for a moment to steady his nerves before walking out of the office and into the chapel itself.

Callie stood at the altar in front of the Elvis impersonator, her hands gripping the small bouquet of rose buds he'd ordered for her. The pale pink of the flowers only highlighted the paleness of her skin. The simple, cream lace sheath dress Bronson had picked out for her gave away nothing of the figure underneath it.

She turned her head when he walked toward her. Chance smiled a little when her eyes widened when she saw her future husband. Chance knew he wasn't unattractive and he hoped it was his looks that made her eyes widen, not the cane he leaned on. The lineup of woman wanting to have a share of his time after a bull ride was testament to the fact that he was popular. But they weren't the type of women he wanted to marry.

For the first time in his life, he wanted a woman he could

depend upon. Someone that wasn't afraid of hard work or getting her hands dirty. It had to be a woman who shared his work ethics and goals who would be more at home helping deliver a calf than she would be clinging to his arm smiling at the press and spending his money. He hoped he'd figured her right. For his plan to work, she needed to be on the same page.

He'd told Callie about his injury. The advertisement stipulated him as a cripple, and the fact he needed help to run the ranch. Perhaps she was expecting someone with more significant injuries, or perhaps it was the scar on his cheek that snaked up through his eyebrow that frightened her. Either way, it was too late for her to back out now. Not after he'd paid to get her this far.

He leaned on the cane and made his way down the aisle toward his new bride. Chance noticed things now he hadn't seen in her grainy profile picture. The small pert nose with its sprinkle of freckles he hadn't picked up on in their Skype chat. The way they dusted over her nose and under her eyelashes. The length of her neck and her petite earlobes devoid of any jewelry. Chance watched the way her brown eyes tilted at the corners giving her an exotic look that spoke of sleepless nights and warm bodies as she watched him hobble toward her.

He'd promised her sex was on the cards as this was going to be a marriage in more than name alone for the time stipulated. After the first twelve months he'd reassess the situation. If his outrageous plan came together, he eventually wanted children and yearned for the day he could teach a youngster of his own to ride and work the ranch. Chance hoped she'd be that woman. He pushed the thought away for now, not keen to bring on bad luck thinking about it. Besides, a man had needs and with a wife who looked like she did, it would be hard to keep his hands to himself.

"Callie." Her eyes widened when he spoke her name. Chance held out a hand and waited for her to take it. She glanced down at it and licked her lips before she placed her tiny hand in his. He gave it a slight squeeze of reassurance. "Ready?"

She nodded and wavered on her feet. Chance dropped her hand and put his arm around her shoulders instead, giving her the support he thought she needed. Elvis cleared his throat and began in his deep southern baritone. "Dearly beloved, we are gathered here today..."

SHE RESTED HER head against the cool glass of the window in the big black truck. They had shared a glass of champagne with Elvis and the two witnesses he'd supplied before signing all the legal paperwork. It was only then that they managed to speak to each other alone.

"Let's get going. It's a long drive back home to the ranch." Chance had taken her hand and gathered the old bag she'd left in the limousine when she'd arrived and hurried her out to the parking lot and into his truck. It wasn't until they were on the road and away from the hustle and bustle of the town that he had spoken to her again.

"You okay? Anything I can get you?"

Callie watched his strong hands gripping the steering wheel and glanced up at his face. The scar was more prominent than she thought it had been in his photograph and the reception had been terrible when they Skyped each other, typical of living in the back of nowhere. She hadn't been very interested in scars when the picture had come through. Why a man as handsome as Chance was would have to advertise for a bride had more than triggered her interest. She'd fired up the old computer at home and Googled him. Nothing came up and she'd wondered why but the temptation of a well-paying contract in exchange for twelve months work had overridden the need to find out. Now Callie knew it was because he didn't go by his real name, at least not the name he'd given her when they were sorting out paperwork. Mitchell Roger Chance Watson. And she'd thought it was because she didn't really know what she was doing. Being computer savvy was her sisters' thing, not hers. Callie preferred to be oblivious to the outside world.

"No, I'm okay. Thank you."

"Now might be the time to ask me some more questions since you didn't seem too interested when we were online. Don't you want to know more about me?"

She sighed and looked across the short distance between them. "Fine. You said you were a cripple but you only use a cane. Seems you're still quite mobile to me. What happened that you needed to go and find a wife with an advertisement instead of the usual way?"

His mouth twisted and he kept his gaze on the road ahead. "Well now." His American drawl prickled her skin sending a shiver up her spine. "I had an accident. Bull by the name of Terror tried his best to kill me. Didn't work but busted my hip up pretty good and left me with a cane and this deadly scar down my face. Ruined my career but that's between us for now. I haven't announced it to my sponsors nor my family yet."

Callie smiled to herself and knew the feeling of keeping secrets, although she wouldn't admit to it, at least not yet. The scar gave him a sinister look she quite liked. Mysterious and intriguing like a dark tortured hero from a movie. "Don't believe in hiding things myself. Still, I'm sure someone with your attributes would have plenty of women after you, and that scar isn't enough in my mind to deter anyone. If anything, it'd only added to the mystery."

"The cane is off-putting. I don't want a sympathy bride."

Her eyebrows shot up. "So why did you mention it in the ad then?" She picked at the broken nail on her hand, rubbing it against her lip before chewing it loose. It all seemed just a little bit dramatic to her. There had to be more to this story than he was telling her. Her life hadn't been super easy up to now, she couldn't see it changing anytime soon so Callie waited for him to tell her the worst.

"I wanted to see if it would put you off. You see, I'm used to people pandering to me because of who I am. I figured if I said I was a crippled rancher who needed hard-working help, it might get me someone who really was interested in me and not my money or my fame."

A mix of emotions rolled around in her stomach. Money and fame. Two things she knew nothing about. But there had to be more to this story. She promised herself to find out eventually and she would. Callie was nothing if not determined. "Gee, thanks for telling me that now."

"Why, would you have come if I'd said I was rich?" He smirked in her direction before looking back at the road.

"Who knows? I have experience with neither so it's all new territory to me. But I don't understand it, why you would want a bride from Australia who now sounds like she won't fit in with your lifestyle? Seems like you could have anyone you wanted if you could get past that chip on our shoulder." She looked at him, trying to figure out what he was hiding from her. "You know why I took the job—I have no money, which I desperately needed and no prospects, but I'm a hard worker."

"I don't have a chip on my shoulder."

"Just telling it how I see it." She looked out the window at the desert.

No point pulling punches with this guy. She wasn't used

to saying things just to make people feel better. Callie couldn't see the point of sugarcoating anything when the truth did just fine.

"Now see, that's exactly why I chose you; your attitude to life. And it's not like you're not easy on the eye. You obviously don't have expensive tastes and high expectations like most of the women I know. You were keen to marry to get security even for a short time, but don't mind working for it, too." He tapped his long fingers on the steering wheel. "I checked you out, Callie. You seem like a nice person and I want a normal life for the next year. I'm sick of the circus being in the public eye is and now my career is over thanks to Terror, who you will meet tomorrow. I want someone who is prepared to work on a marriage and a life. I don't know any women who would be prepared to take that on with me unable to do as much as I'm expecting from you."

She glanced at him. "What did you do?"

"I was a bull rider on the IBR tour. Did really well for myself, too, but the last accident was the one that ended that career for good."

"I'm sorry to hear that. Surely you must have friends who could help you out though, or family. Seems kind of extreme to me to marry someone just for that."

"My brothers have their own lives. I don't expect them to drop everything to help me while letting their own places slide backwards. Besides, I have breeding program worked out and I need to be there to oversee it. I need you to be my legs until I can cope on my own if that will ever happen." He took a deep breath. "And in return, you get a handsome payout with a bonus if you manage to raise the stock levels by twenty percent as I said in the agreement."

"You told me it was only for one year." Callie swallowed. It was too late for pride to rear its ugly head. She'd already banked the first check and paid out most of the family's more urgent debts. The bank would come after her for more sooner or later but, for now, they were happy with what she'd given them.

"It is, but we may find that we need more time to set the scene for our divorce. I don't want to tell my family yet that I've married you. There are things I need to deal with first, one thing at a time."

"Fine." She fought the panic rising in her throat. Could she cope being in a marriage with this man for that long, away from her sisters? But more time would mean more money, right? It might be to her benefit in more ways than one but still, the twins were so far away and she missed them already. *Take it for the team, Callie. You know you have, too.* Practical to the end, she knew she had no choice.

"I promise you won't suffer from any extra time you spend here. I'll make sure of it."

"Thanks. I appreciate it."

The sun started to disappear behind a cloud and she rubbed her arms as goose bumps fluttered over her skin. The dress wasn't warm enough for the cool of the day as it got closer to late afternoon.

"Here," Chance hooked his jacket from over the back of his seat and pushed it toward her. "Put this on, it gets pretty cool out here from midafternoon on. Do you have anything warm in your bag? You didn't bring many clothes with you."

"I don't have much. Never saw the point of it really, being as it is so hot in Australia where we lived and my life was spent on the farm. Just a couple pairs of jeans, and shirts, and my work boots. Never had reason for a pretty dress like this one."

"We'll drive until it's dark and then find a motel on the highway. Once we get closer to the ranch I'll stop and you can get some more clothes. No point freezing your butt off out here. Snow's still on the hills."

She smiled, whipping her head around to look at him. "Snow. Really? I've never seen it, apart from on the television."

"It can be beautiful but, then again, it can be deadly out here. Not much fun getting caught out in a blizzard so you need to be careful. Damnedest things always happen around then too. A cow will go and calf right when the worst hits so we gotta go bring them in or risk losing the calf."

"Don't you bring them closer to the home paddock when they're about to calf? It's what we do." She looked out over the hills and the wide open spaces and sighed at the amount of rich green grass she saw. What they wouldn't give to have this in Australia instead of being permanently stuck in a drought.

"Yes, we do, but it doesn't always work out. Seems at least once a season there'll be some old girl who just slips away to do her own thing when she thinks nobody is looking. Truth be told, she's usually alright but not always. I've had different people looking after the place while I've been out on the tour with good and bad results. Now I'm not able to anymore"—he gestured to his bad leg—"it's up to you and me to do the best we can with the place."

"Right. So is that leg going to get any better or is that what you're left with?" She looked at the cane wondering if it was going to be a permanent fixture in their lives.

"Would it worry you if it was?" His dark eyes bored into hers.

"No. Just asking. I mean if you need to have me do physio or anything like that, I think you're out of luck. Never was that good at massaging or anything like that." She thought over her words and blushed. *Idiot!* Callie turned back to the window, hiding her flaming cheeks from Chance. She could hear his soft laugh and wanted to crawl under the seat.

"I have to go back into the hospital in a few weeks to get the pins out of my hip, but Doc doesn't see me getting much more mobile than I am right now." He paused for a moment. "I'm sure when the cold sets in a massage would probably be just what I need to keep the movement up. It tends to get sore when it's cold."

"That's a shame, for you I mean. Must be hard to take

after the life you've led." She ignored the massage reference, preferring not to think of him half naked and under her hands. Not a blushing virgin, Callie still hadn't had many lovers and the thought of seeing this hunky cowboy in the nude was tempting and enough to make her girly bits stand up and take notice. Sex was on the cards and the thought took flight now she knew how cute and considerate he really was.

"It wasn't pleasant to wake up to." He kept his eyes on the road and Callie settled down to a quiet ride. She had just nodded off when the truck pulled into a motel parking lot and she jolted awake. The neon red lights on the roof flashed off and on advertising vacant rooms. She tried to wake herself up but when Chance put his hand on her shoulder and told her to stay where she was for a bit longer, she closed her eyes again and let herself drift off to another place.

The cool air startled her and she opened her eyes as Chance opened the door of the truck. "Come on, Callie. Time for bed."

Bed? I had hoped I could get to know you first before we did that. Like in a normal relationship. The words tumbled through her brain as she struggled to wake up. He held out his hand while she slid down out of the truck. She held his jacket closer to her body and looked at the partially open door of the motel room in front of them. Slowly she followed her new husband inside. The large bed sat in the center of the room with a couple of armchairs to one side. A big television screen had been mounted in the middle of the wall and a tiny fridge was tucked under a counter top where Chance placed her bag.

When he turned away and walked back outside, she glanced around, poking her nose into the small en suite they would have to share.

He shut the door behind him. "You go first if you want. I'm going to sit down and put my leg up for a bit. Maybe have a beer." He threw his bag beside hers and rubbed his hip before ambling over to an armchair. "I ordered a meal to be delivered so we don't have to go out. Figured a quiet night was in order after today"

"Thanks. Um, do you want me to do anything for you, get you some painkillers or something?"

"No, but thanks for the offer. I've got it covered."

She hurried over to her holdall, opened it, and took out her bathroom bag along with a set of clean clothing she could sleep in. She slammed the door shut behind her and sagged against it. This was all a very bad idea. Moving to another country to marry a man she'd never met was bordering on pathologically unsafe and insane. But at the time she saw his ad, there had been no other option and she couldn't bear to tell her grandparents how bad things really were. Even she had been staggered at the size of the debt her parents had accrued keeping the farm going. The last thing she wanted to do was ask for money when they'd already offered to bring up her sisters and her if she'd wanted to move to the city.

Connecting with her maternal grandparents wasn't really an option either, no matter what she'd told her grandfather. She had no idea who they were and if they were even still alive. Not that she would go begging for money from them anyway. They'd never shown a scrap of interest in her or her sisters from what she could understand, so why would they help out now when their daughter was dead and buried in another country?

She looked at her reflection in the mirror over the white porcelain sink. Her eyes had shadows underneath them and her skin was pasty white under the fluorescent lights. Callie was tired and hungry, but the main problem was her nerves. This was her wedding night and, whether she liked it or not, she had to consummate the marriage sooner or later. It was in the contract she signed before Chance bought her ticket and paid lifesaving money into her bank account. She twirled the ring around on her finger, looking at the wide platinum band studded with tiny diamonds. It looked out of place on her normally dirty, scuffed knuckles. Her hands were tanned and strong, but it was the chewed and broken nails she focused on. Cattle and horses never cared if she had a manicure and not being a girly girl, it'd never been high on her list of priorities. Her husband had brought home a farming girl from the outback, where as she would have thought he'd be more suited to someone that moved in the same circles he did. One that was used to flashy hotel rooms and butler service and fine jewelry.

She unzipped her bathroom bag and took out a tooth-brush and toothpaste, squirting a long line on the bristles. Callie put it in her mouth and mindlessly brushed away, wondering how she was going to get out of having sex tonight.

Chapter Four

THE LOOK OF panic in her eyes told Chance his new wife was not looking forward to sharing his bed this evening even though on paper it was part of the agreement. She'd made a deal and he was going to make her stick to it eventually. Besides, he was intrigued with her. He still couldn't believe she'd gone through with the deal. Hell, he couldn't quite believe he'd advertised for a wife either. There had to be other ways to convince the wider public he wasn't marriage material but so far he hadn't found it. For the last week he'd been sure she would renege on the agreement and he would be out of pocket for her expenses plus the wallop of cash he'd deposited in her bank account. Credit to her for sticking to her side of the bargain.

The search he'd done on her had brought up more than he had expected. Left with no parents and twin sisters to raise after her parents had been killed in an automobile accident, it seemed as though Callie had no option but to take a risk on him. The debt recovery notices out on her family home were enough to make him worry she would take the money and run, but she hadn't. She'd arrived at the hotel and settled in for a night, albeit a little out of her comfort zone.

Bronson, the butler from the hotel, had called him to let him know she was well and he would have her at the chapel the following day at the correct time. It paid to have friends amongst the places he frequented often. Sadly, now that wouldn't happen but he didn't regret his decision to put all of his energies into getting the ranch working to full capacity and saying goodbye to the life of a playboy.

His manager and the officials at the International Bull Riders were devastated understandably but that was life on the tour and they'd seen it all before. Cowboys got hurt and had to find another career. His happened sooner than any of them thought but that was the way it went. He'd still be working for them in a mentoring capacity because of his experience and high profile so it wasn't as though he was cutting his ties altogether. His ranch was going to be home from now on all year round. Chance's mind had been buzzing for weeks with his new breeding program and what he could achieve back home in Marietta.

Having the farming experience and the degree in stock management she had, Callie would be very handy to have around. She wasn't after him for his status or money. His money—well, yes, to an extent, but he'd gone into that deal willingly once he'd seen her profile picture and read her story. And he would have offered the same proposition to anyone who took his fancy and kept the deal a secret from the public. But more than anything, he wanted someone honest and down-to-earth, and what better way than to place an ad for a hard worker and a wife and get to vet them before they had a chance to profess their love. He'd been caught too many times already to risk having his dreams dashed again.

He rubbed at his hip, wishing the long drive home was already over. A good night's sleep in his own bed called to him, but the thought of flying in and out of Las Vegas to save time had made his skin crawl. Once one of his favorite haunts, being there today had shown him how much he had changed in the last few months, knowing his time in the public eye was over. It was like shutting a door on his other life and not having any qualms about doing it, which he was finding hard to believe. Getting back home and showing Callie around, introducing her to his brothers, and exploring the ranch with her was foremost in his mind now. After a good night's sleep and some pain relief.

It seemed she spent a long time in the bathroom. Their dinner arrived and there was still no sign of her. Chance went and knocked on the door. "Callie, dinner is here."

She emerged with a pair of track pants and an old T-shirt on. Her hair was damp and pulled up into a messy knot on the back of her head, and her face appeared drawn and pale. He wanted to scrape back the missed strands of hair and tuck them behind her ear.

"Eat up and then we can get an early night. It's still a

fairly big drive tomorrow."

"Thanks, but I'm not really that hungry." She hugged her arms around her body and Chance noticed the perky nipples under the thin cotton of her threadbare shirt. His body reacted appropriately and he shifted his hips to get more comfortable.

"You have to eat. You're supposed to look after me, remember? How can you do that if you don't eat enough to feed a prairie dog?" She blushed charmingly under his scrutiny. "Sit down and dig in. I don't bite."

A small table had been moved to between the armchairs and covered trays were place on either side of it. He watched Callie sit down and lift the cover from her meal. She sniffed as the steam from the fried chicken and gravy wafted from the plate. A small smile touched her lips and interest sparked in her eyes. "Smells pretty good."

"Tastes good, too. Can't beat a plate of fried chicken and gravy. Unless it's a good steak that is." He sat down and lifted the cover from his own plate and picked up his knife and fork. The first mouthful was heaven on his tongue. Crispy fried chicken and mashed potatoes drenched in rich brown gravy had the ability to make his taste buds stand up and pay attention every single time. A good, wholesome meal.

Chance watched her devour the plate of food from the corner of his eye and smiled to himself. He hated a woman who denied herself a decent meal to garner the look of a half-starved waif because she thought it was the in thing. Callie was muscled but still managed to look stick thin. He figured a good bout of sickness would have her fading away to nothing. Fattening her up a little just became top priority for him. It would be nice to see her curves fill out and the paleness leave her face. Nothing wrong with hard work in his mind but one had to fuel the body right to keep it going without suffering a serious case of crash and burn. He wasn't about to let his new wife fade away to nothing.

"Good wasn't it?" He smiled as she wiped the final dregs of gravy from her plate with the small dinner roll. She put it in her mouth and leaned back in the chair, her eyes closed in pleasure as she chewed on the final bite. As she swallowed, Chance glanced at her from under his lashes, mesmerized by how her throat worked, and heat simmered in his gut. She was gorgeous. The most natural woman he'd seen in a long time. No vestige of makeup marred her skin on their wedding day and she had no airs and graces that he could see so far. A simple, down-to-earth girl who would fit in at the ranch with him to make the place something to be proud of. He hoped.

"Very. You were right, I needed that." Callie glanced in his direction and he watched the heat race up her cheeks.

"Go to bed, Callie. I'm not an animal so don't worry that I'm going to force you tonight. We have plenty of time to figure out what works for us."

He saw the relief as a long breath shuddered from her

body and her shoulders slumped. A quick sheen of tears filled her eyes and she lifted a hand to her mouth, biting down on the skin of her fingers. Chance twisted in his chair as far as his bad hip would allow and reached over to take her hand.

"You should've said something. You sounded so brave over the internet when we sorted out the rules of engagement for this marriage."

She lifted huge, frightened eyes to him. The green flecks in the pools of earthy brown reminded him of the colors in the trees at the base of the mountains in autumn when the leaves changed before they dropped to the ground.

"It's not the idea of having sex with you. I'm prepared for that. I was kind of hoping we could get to know each other first like in a normal relationship."

"This is anything but normal. Are you saying you don't want to go ahead with that part of the deal?"

"No, of course not. I like sex as much as the next person and what's not to like about you? I mean, check out the mirror, Chance. You're every girl's favorite cowboy." She smiled. "I needed the money so badly I would've agreed to anything." She looked at him defiantly, her chin raised and stubborn. Her Australian drawl seemed more intensified when she was emotional or tired and Chance could listen to her voice forever. He wondered if she knew how easy she was to read, or maybe it was just that he was becoming attuned to her moods.

"You need to promise me something. I want the truth

between us, even when it hurts." He ran his calloused thumb across the palm of her hand, feeling the ridges of tough skin from hard work. "This deal has to work for both of us. We went into it for a reason, didn't we?"

She nodded her head. "I just don't know if we can make it work. I'm not sure we should even try. Keep this more as a business deal where neither of us gets hurt at the end of it."

"The thing is, I want a wife and it has to be one I can rely on. Not someone just in name alone. You won't just be a ranch hand, Callie. You'll be my partner in all things including my bed when we both feel you're ready. We won't be able to convince anyone we're truly married it we sleep in separate beds. At the end of the contract, we can decide what to do from there."

She tossed her head, sending the now dry tendrils of hair from her face. "I still don't see why you did this. I mean, I know now that you're someone special or at least a little bit famous and you can fill me in on all that later. So I really don't get it. You could have had anyone. Why me, really, since we're all about telling the truth?"

"Because I'm not who people think I am. I don't want to have to keep up the façade any longer." He squeezed her fingers once more before letting go of her hand. Chance sat up in the chair, shifting slightly to ease the pain in his hip. He couldn't bear the look in her eyes if he told her the truth about why he avoided a serious relationship. He'd been slapped down before and he wasn't going to risk it again.

Not yet.

"Who are you then?" Callie curled her feet up under her body and watched him, no longer wary of him.

"I had a fabulous early childhood growing up but that changed when my mother died. My father couldn't cope and turned to the bottle to get through every day." He vowed never to put his children through the same thing. "It was hard on me and my brothers. Granddad tried to help us but he was pushed away, told not to interfere. I tried to shield the boys as much as I could to start with because I was the loudest I guess, especially after Evan went to med school. The more our father drank, the harder it got. One day he took a swing at me and I couldn't take it anymore. I hit back, then I left. I walked out and didn't look back, something I'm not proud of. I couldn't stay living at home, not getting anywhere. I needed the money the IBR would give me to help set them up with a decent chance of life since our father was intent on drinking away every dollar he earned."

She rested her chin on her hand and watched him.

The familiar hollowness ached in his gut; a small reminder of the guilt he'd carried around for years at leaving his brothers behind. "I didn't care if he drank himself into an early grave, but I should have stayed for my brothers. They had nobody to look after them and I've never forgiven myself for that."

"Hmm, sounds to me like you never had a choice. What would have happened if you stayed? Couldn't your grandfather help? Ours took my sisters in, offered me a place, too."

"That wasn't possible for us. Would have caused too much of a drift amongst the family and the boys wanted to stay with our father anyway. Seemed I was the only one who hated him for what he did. Who knows what might have been? My youngest brother Tyson told me later that the old man was mad fit to bust and it was probably for the best I went when I did, but that still doesn't excuse the fact that I thought of myself first and left them to fend with him themselves."

"Did they forgive you?" Her eyes swam with sympathy.

"Yeah. It's me who has the issues with it all, not them."

"So what's the problem here then? You still haven't answered the question."

Chance looked at her wondering if he'd gotten more than he bargained for with Callie. She was like a dog with a bone. "When I ran away, I had to stand up for myself and I figured the best way to do that was to reinvent myself, so Chance the cocky bull rider was born. There wasn't anything I wouldn't try at least once. I mixed with anyone who could get me higher up the professional ladder. I made sure I was always in the public eye and used people for my own gain."

"You mean like famous people?"

"Yeah. Fake it 'til you make it kind of thing. Eventually I was more famous than I could have thought and I found I really didn't like it. I made sure the press noticed me every chance I got and women threw themselves at me. It got kind of old pretty quick."

"But it paid off obviously." A small smile lifted the corners of her mouth and he could see the sparkle in her eyes.

"Of course it did. I was at the top of my game, I had my own business plan and money wasn't a problem. I managed to help my brothers out and when Pop died, he left me the ranch. Life was good." He gave a bitter laugh.

"Until Terror."

"Yeah, until Terror did the deed on me. My own stupid fault, I know that. Maybe it was my subconscious telling me it was time to quit and go back to what I really wanted, who knows. But when I woke up in hospital with my hip pinned together, I knew it was my opportunity to let go of the wild life even if I didn't want to face up to that reality. It took me quite some time to come to terms with where my life was going."

"So what's wrong with that then? I don't understand. I mean I get that you were putting on a false front for the public and everything to achieve your goals, but why is it a problem now? Can't you just fade away into your own life?"

"That's the general plan, but it's going to take some work and it might impact on you to some extent."

"I don't get it." She frowned. "Why would it?"

"Everyone thinks I like the high life, including my brothers. I doubt anyone would believe I suddenly turned into a diehard rancher who wants to be left alone away from the fame and money I used to live with."

"Who cares what people think?"

"My brothers don't know yet I can't ride anymore." Chance pushed himself to his feet, his hip aching from sitting in the hard chair. "Plus I have my sponsors to think of. I've been very lucky so far. I've managed to build my brand with my own range of products that sell well. I want that to continue."

"Like what, aftershave or something?" She grinned as she said it.

"Yes, aftershave. I also have a line of whiskey, clothing and boots, a range of sauces and barbeques. We're bringing out grill utensils this fall as well to coincide with the next tour."

"That's pretty cool. I suck at cooking so I'm not likely to have even heard about them." She yawned and held a hand up to her mouth. "When are you telling your family then?"

"Not sure. They think I've just gone to the airport to pick up a farm manager and then I'll be back on the tour once my hip is healed. It's not like this is the first injury I've had. We tend to get hurt on a regular basis but this is the first serious one. I think they figure I'm indestructible."

"So they don't know you married me or why then?" She shrugged her shoulders. "Just tell them the truth."

"Now there lies the problem. If they find out I did it all for them because I felt guilty, how do you think they'll feel?"

Her mouth opened in a round "O". Callie looked at him with realization dawning. "They can think I'm just the ranch manager, fine. But how do you think you're going to pull this off? I mean, you'll have to tell them sooner or later you can't go back to the tour. Surely they would understand that."

"Yes, they would, and that's still plenty of time away yet but they wouldn't understand me marrying a quiet, country girl and retiring to the mountains to raise bulls, and I don't want to have to go into the whole contract thing with them. Not their business anyway. They'd expect me to marry someone famous and stay in the limelight. It's just how I spent the last twelve years of my life and it would be too much of a change for me to pull it off otherwise."

"So what do we do now?"

"I want you to pretend to be the farm manager for a while. Let me ease them into it. Once they get used to you and see me happy back on the ranch, I can tell them." He tried to smile at her but it came off as a grimace. "I know it sounds weak, but I don't want to make them feel responsible for the way my life turned out. I feel bad enough leaving them with a drunk for a father without them thinking I put up with all the crap I did to make up for it. Double whammy if you get me."

"Would they even be there at the ranch that often?" Callie picked at the fingernail she'd pulled off earlier, her gaze steady on his face.

"Yeah, Tyson can't seem to stay away. Even Rory who lives about nine hours away pops in for a day here and there when the mood takes him and he feels like a drive. He lost his wife a few years ago and is having trouble being anywhere near the rest of the family for more than a day or so a year."

"That's sad."

"Yeah, but it's his choice so I can't push my ideas on him. I'm sure eventually he'll come around."

CALLIE STOOD, STRETCHED and yawned again. "I need sleep. Which side is better for you?" She looked at the bed and her eyes almost drooped in relief.

"I'm happy either side. Take your pick."

She walked over and pulled back the covers, plumping up the pillows. "So, does that mean we share a room when we get home or what?"

"Sure, just not when my brothers come over. You can set yourself up in one of the guest rooms to keep the illusion of ranch manager rolling." He hobbled over to the bed. "Callie, I appreciate it, I really do. I know I got you over here under slightly false pretentions to some extent but it'll work out, I promise, and you'll still get your money at the end of it."

"I can hardly blame you for what you did when I've only come over here for the money. too. Guess we both have our demons, but I'm no sorrier than you are for doing it. My sisters are relying on me to clear the farm's debts and provide for them when they finish school." She climbed into bed and snuggled down with the blankets pulled up under her arms. "I couldn't do it without you making this offer."

"So you have no issues sleeping with me then?" Chance looked down on her and she lifted a hand to shield her eyes.

"I agreed, didn't I? I don't like the idea of selling myself but people have been in worse situations." She heaved out a sigh. "Look, just so you know, I'm not a prude, but if we can do this by telling ourselves we're only friends with benefits, that will make it easier for me. But I did go on the pill so we don't get caught out getting pregnant because that sure wouldn't work into the plan."

"Yeah, good idea and I appreciate it. Well, I'm going to have a shower and crash. Tomorrow is another big drive." He hobbled toward the bathroom and shut the door behind him.

Callie let out a sigh of relief. He deserved what he'd paid for and if truth be told it wouldn't be a hardship to sleep with him. She hadn't been with anyone for ages and besides, she was going to make sure she kept her side of the bargain. She clicked off the bedside lamp and snuggled deeper into the pillow, closing her eyes.

Callie was almost asleep when Chance came out of the bathroom. He left the light on behind him and closed the door leaving a one inch gap for light during the night. She watched him limp toward the bed illuminated from the light behind him. A white towel hung low around his hips, showing off the shape of a well-toned body that got her heart rate moving up a notch or two. She kept her breathing even and her eyes closed to a slit.

When he pulled back the cover, Chance dropped the towel to the floor and shuffled between the sheets. She heard the intake of breath as he tried to get comfortable. Unsure of whether to offer him help or ignore it for now, Callie held still and waited to see what happened before she did anything.

Within minutes his breathing changed to a deeper pace and she realized he was already asleep. She relaxed and rolled over onto her back. Through the curtains, the red neon light still flashed, illuminating the dark night sky and warning drivers of the available rooms. The rumble of semitrucks driving through town broke the still night as they passed. The sky hovered between grey and black when she finally fell asleep.

THE SMOOTH CHEST under her hand was warm and inviting. Callie rubbed her fingertips over the small nub of flesh and snuggled closer, the male smell holding her close. A firm hand cupped her butt and pulled her closer still, another hand stroked the hair from her face. She snuggled her cheek into the rough palm, feeling secure and relaxed for the first time in months.

Callie opened her eyes and squealed. Chance held her

tight and her arms were wrapped around his naked body, her legs twined with his.

"Stay there. You feel good like this." His eyes were closed and there was a small smile twitching the corners of his full mouth. Callie relaxed. "And stop overthinking this. Just relax for a few more moments and then we need to get up and on the road."

She swallowed and looked at the face within licking distance. His blond hair was cut fairly short but still curled around his ears and a cowlick graced the corner of his forehead. A day's growth showed through the golden tan of his skin, leaving a soft cast of shadow around his chin and over his top lip. The scar ran from his cheek through his eyebrow and snaked up to the parting in his hair. It had faded but she could see the tiny points where the stitches had been placed and her fingers itched to touch them.

Long golden eyelashes wavered and she wondered what it would be like to have them flutter against her cheek.

"Stop thinking and lie still. Relax, woman."

Callie obeyed and let her head drop back to his shoulder, snuggling into his chest. The woodsy smell of his aftershave still lingered on his skin, reminding her of pine forests and rushing streams of cool clear water and she wondered if it was his own brand. Something for her to think about instead of the naked body she was tucked into.

"You tossed and turned all night. Was it that bad a day yesterday?" His lashes opened and he looked down at her with soft blue, cloudless eyes.

"Yes and no. It's going to be a challenge for both of us, but we're both doing it for good reasons. I don't want my sisters to grow up thinking my folks didn't care enough about them to make provision for when they're older." She swallowed and pushed away the emotion that rushed up her throat whenever she thought of her parents. "They deserve more than that, I think."

"Exactly how I felt about my brothers and why I did what I did. We're not that different when you think about it. We can make this work, Callie. I know we can." He pushed her back on the pillow and raised himself over her.

"Chance—" Her words were cut off when his lips came down over hers.

She sucked in a breath and the taste of him rolled over her tongue. He nipped at her top lip and looked down into her eyes. Before she could say anything he dipped down to her mouth again, this time running his tongue over the curve of her top lip. Callie tried to grasp his tongue with her teeth but he evaded her.

Her eyes closed as he latched onto her lips, pushing his tongue into her mouth to trace the ridges of her teeth. She paused, eager to respond but wary of letting this get out of control so soon. His body covered hers and she thrust up, her hips moving of their own accord, a reminder it had been far too long since her body had been tempted to let go.

Callie wrapped her hand around the back of his neck,

gripping tightly to keep him where he was. Her body took over from her mind and she hooked a leg over his, one hand running down his back and cupping his firm, naked butt.

He gasped and a moan escaped his throat.

"Sorry, oh, Chance, I'm so stupid." Her heart ached to see him screwing up his face in pain.

He rested his forehead on hers, breathed through his mouth and kept his eyes closed until the pain receded. With a deep steadying breath, he opened his eyes and looked into hers. "Sorry, not your fault." He kissed her again and eased himself back to rest on the pillow, a hand draped over his face.

"No, I should have known better. You've been hurt badly and I kind of forgot there for a minute." Heat raced up her cheeks and she sat up, wrapping her arms around her knees. "If I'd stuck to the plan it wouldn't have happened."

He reached out a hand, placing it on her back. "Don't torment yourself. I never expected you to react that way or I would've waited until I was feeling better." He chuckled and she risked a peek over her shoulder at him. He burst out laughing and Callie frowned, thinking she was the butt of a private joke.

"What is so damned funny, cowboy?" She shuffled around, rose to her knees, and glared at him, her hands on her hips as she towered over him threateningly.

"You and me. Who would have thought a mail order wedding would have us reacting like this to each? I want you as much as you want me. You can't deny it after that reaction."

"How can I when I was just climbing all over you? If you hadn't yelped like a girl, we would be cozy by now." She smiled and scurried off the bed. "Time to get a move on if we want to get home tonight, wouldn't you say?"

She grabbed her clothes bag and hurried to the bathroom, slamming the door behind her before he was out of bed. She fanned herself and moaned, holding her thighs tightly together. How bad was that? Or good, depending on which way she looked at it. To get saddled with a guy who didn't turn her on was one of the things that scared her the most, which was why she'd reacted the way she had last night. Nothing wrong with sex. It was a healthy part of life and the gorgeous hunk was her husband after all. At least for now. Might as well make the most of it. She'd already promised herself to do anything she could to make the guy like her and the time spent together easy but she hadn't expected to get so lucky quite so quick.

Callie squeezed her eyes shut and fist pumped the air. *Yes!* That hot cowboy was hers, and all she had to do was pretend he wasn't when there was anyone around until they had the rest of the family eased into his new way of life. Shouldn't be too hard to do. A quick thought sobered her. What would happen when she had to let him go?

There was a tap on the door.

"Hang on." She hurried into a pair of comfy, worn jeans

and button up shirt and ran her fingers through her hair.

Once her teeth were brushed, she checked her reflection in the mirror. There was color to her cheeks that wasn't there yesterday. Thank goodness that day was over and done with. Now to get into the swing of things as the wife of the hunkiest cowboy she'd ever laid eyes on.

Callie pulled open the bathroom door and stopped. Chance was standing with a towel around his hips and a smile on his face, one arm on the door frame. Her stomach plummeted.

Chapter Five

T HE STARTLED LOOK on her face changed as soon as she gathered herself. She leaned against the door and pursed her lips. "So, the plan for today would be?" Her cute Aussie accent would slay the locals, he was sure of it.

"How about I have five minutes in here to do my thing and you order us breakfast and see if they'll deliver it for us?" The swell of her breasts under the old, cotton shirt threatened to make him ignore the pain and take her back to bed.

Who could have imagined he would fall for the petite Australian farmer as quickly as he had? Certainly not him. He'd better be careful not to show her his true feelings.

Callie licked her lips and he watched her gaze roam his naked chest. "I guess I could do that."

"I would prefer to do something else myself. I think it would be advisable to wait until we get home, though. At least there's a much more comfortable bed which would ease the pain on my hip since I'm sure it's going to get a workout. I don't like taking too many painkillers when I have to drive so far."

"Um, well…" She stood up and tucked her hands behind her back. "Yeah, that might be a good idea. I can always drive you know. Give you a break along the way if you like." She gazed up at him with such earnest eyes he was reminded of an innocence lacking for too long in his life.

"I might take you up on that. Breakfast first and then we can hit the highway."

Callie ducked out under his arm and hurried over to the phone to call the restaurant next door for breakfast.

"One more thing."

She looked over her shoulder at him.

"Your wedding ring. Can you take it off and hide it until we sort this out with the family?"

A shadow passed over her eyes and she nodded her head then turned to pick up the phone. Chance heard her voice as he shut the door.

An hour later they were in the truck, eating up the miles toward home.

"Tell me about your brothers. How many do you have and what do they do?" She tucked a leg up under her butt and turned to watch him.

"Well now, there's Tyson, the youngest. He lives on the ranch next door to me. Horses are his thing, especially stock horses. You know about Rory. He really has had it pretty tough." Chance shook his head and checked in the rear vision mirror. "He married quite young, which was fine because he and his wife were made for each other. Everyone could see it. She was the sweetest thing and he adored her."

"What happened to her?"

Chance glanced at her, while she took in everything he said. "She was on the way home from a doctor's appointment. Rory thinks she was distracted because she'd just found out she was having a baby. Never saw the truck or the stop sign and sailed right through it."

"That's terrible. The poor things." Her eyes misted over and Chance could have kicked himself. Her parents died in a car accident, too. It must bring it all back. "I'm sorry. I shouldn't have said that."

"No, it's okay. It happened. Nothing's going to change that, same as nothing is going to change it for Rory. Doesn't he want to move on and get on with life?"

"Not really. He's very bitter about it all. The others have both tried to get him to move closer so we can help him out but he won't fall in with the plan. Reckons he's better off being miserable by himself."

"I can understand that. Maybe he'll come around soon. How many more in the family?"

"Well, there's Evan. He's in Dallas right now. I know he's hoping to come home and open his own medical practice once he has a bit more experience. Not sure I would be too happy having him poking around with me, but that's 'cause he's my brother. Not saying his skills aren't any good. Passed his exams with flying colors so I guess someone trusts him."

Callie laughed, poking him in the arm. "That is so mean. How could you talk like that about your brother?"

" 'Cause he's my brother, that's exactly why. You didn't know him as a kid like I did. Playing doctors with him was never any fun, let me tell you."

"Hmmm, I don't believe you for one minute. Where does your dad live?"

A cold chill crept up his spine and he glance away out the driver's side window. "He lives in town still. In the old house we've lived in since I was born. You won't be seeing anything of him."

They drove on for the next few miles in silence. When a gas station came into view, Chance pulled over. "You might want a bathroom stop or a drink. I may as well fuel up and it will get us home." He jumped out of his seat and, leaning on the truck for support, reached for the fuel hose.

He heard the other door open and then the tap of feet on the pavement. Chance watched as Callie walked over to the service station door and went inside. Her worn jeans hugged her shapely butt like a second skin. As much as he liked them, she would need warmer clothes before they got to the ranch. Alice Springs in Australia was a lot hotter that Montana ever got. With the snow on the mountains all year round, it was colder than Callie would be used to. And even with spring under way, it would still be colder than she could imagine.

CALLIE PUSHED OPEN the door to the restroom and hurried to an empty stall. It stood to reason Chance would be sensitive about his father but, at the end of the day, he was still his father. If her mother had been the only one killed in the accident she could easily imagine her dad turning to the bottle. He'd loved her so much. He would've been devastated without her. A love like that would be hard to get over. She'd just have to remember to tread carefully there when the subject came up. Maybe one day she would get to meet her father-in-law and decide for herself if he was a nice person or not. She did her business and washed her hands before venturing out to the shop. Chance stood at the counter, paying for the gas, and gestured to her. "Want anything to eat? A coffee to go?"

"Coffee would be great, thanks." She waited beside him until he'd paid and she took the take-out cup he offered her, grabbing his as well so he could use his cane. Together they walked back to the truck and she passed his cup over once they were back on the road again.

"Didn't mean to bite your head off over the old man. Bit of a sore point."

"Fair enough. So, is that it then? Tyson, Rory and Evan?"

"Yeah. Don't you think that's enough for me to put up with?"

"Sounds like you guys clash." She sipped her coffee and watched the road ahead.

"Don't pull punches, do you? Is it an Australian thing?" Chance glanced at her and she smiled.

"Could be, or it might just be me. Never did see the point in spouting off bull shit just to make someone happy. I tell it like it is, cowboy."

He roared with laughter. "Makes me wonder if I've bitten off more than I was expecting somehow."

"Too late now, I've spent the first check."

"Did it make much difference?"

"Yeah, it did. The bank gave me the breathing space now to sort out the rest of the debts. Not that I can do much more for a while, but at least it's a start."

"I can sort out those bills, Callie. I have more money than I know what to do with and we can take it out at the other end if you like. Won't make much difference to me."

"No! Thanks, but no. You've already done enough and with the wage you want to pay me on top of it, that's more than I would get anywhere else."

"Your call. Just remember it's there and, as my wife, you have the right to ask me for anything you want. Regardless of the pre-nup you signed, I won't see you go without something if it's important."

"Thanks." She sipped her coffee and looked out the window, soaking up the view as they drove home.

Chapter Six

THE SMALL TOWN of Marietta came into view and Chance eased off the gas. He always relaxed when he made it this close to his ranch. The tension slid from his shoulders and he could breathe easier when he knew he was only minutes from home. He drove through Main Street and pulled up in front of Marietta Western Wear. Callie needed more clothes and this was the easiest place to get everything she would require.

"Come on. Let's go shopping." Chance opened his door and slid out, taking his cane with him. He waited for Callie to get out of the truck. She seemed reluctant to go inside, looking at the display in the window with a frown.

"You need more than what you brought with you. We're still not completely out of winter yet, and even when spring sets in properly, it doesn't get anywhere near as hot as what you're used to in the desert. We could get a good dumping in the next few weeks. There's nothing like a spring storm surprising us like they do on occasion. Those clothes aren't going to keep you warm enough." He placed a hand on the small of her back and pushed her toward the door.

The bell tinkled overhead as they walked in the shop.

"Chance. Nice to see you. What can I do for you today?" A rosy-cheeked, elderly lady with her hair done in a bun on the top of her head ambled toward them, her hands clasped around a portly belly.

"Hi, Sue Ellen. This is Callie, she's come to help run the ranch for me. Needs a whole wardrobe. Can I leave her in your capable hands to fit her out for me?"

"Chance…" Callie turned to him, her eyes pleading.

"Well now, I think I can manage that. Guessing you want the whole shooting match then; boots, shoes and the like. Been right cold these last couple of days." She glanced up and down at Callie and raised an eyebrow in Chance's direction.

"Yes. Everything and make sure she has a decent jacket, too. Can't have her out in the terrible weather, freezing her butt off when she has to feed out. Give her a hat, too. I'll be back in an hour or so. You ladies have fun now." He winked at Callie and left her standing with Sue Ellen knowing he was going to get a talking to when he came back.

"Well now." He heard Sue Ellen saying as he shut the door and headed up the road to take care of other business.

"THERE, THAT SHOULD do you. Can't think of anything I've

missed." Sue Ellen glanced at the bags piled up on the counter and rubbed her hands together. "So, you came all the way from Australia to work for Chance?"

"Yes." Callie wished the floor would open up and swallow her whole. The woman had asked question after question, never seeming satisfied with Callie's answers.

"Reckon it's his business, but don't rightly seem like the thing to do when young Jethro was looking for work. Put in a good offer, too, he did from what he tells me. What on earth was Chance thinking hiring someone as frail looking as you? Reckon a strong headwind will knock you flying."

"I'm stronger than I look but, if you have any issues with me being here, perhaps you should ask him that. I'm only an employee after all." She was getting tired of the questions and just wished he would come back and save her.

"A very well looked after employee from what I can see. Right, let me ring this lot up and see what Chance owes me." Sue Ellen started the long task of going through every item and loading it into the old fashioned cash register.

When the doorbell tinkled, Callie turned, breathing a sigh of relief. Chance walked in, a smile on his face. "So, we're ready to go then?"

"Just give me a minute to tally this up and it's all yours."

Chance leaned on the counter and gazed at Callie, a lazy smile on his face. She frowned at him and turned away. Once they were out of this shop he was going to get an earful. She brought her own clothes, and this was just plain embarrassing. Made her feel like a kept woman, which she was. Didn't mean she had to like it.

"Here you go." Sue Ellen handed him a slip of paper and Chance signed it before handing it back with his credit card.

"Thanks, Sue Ellen, appreciate it. Grab some bags and let's get going."

Callie scrambled to grab the purchases and hustled them out to the truck. She piled them all onto the back seat and climbed up in the front, jamming her seat belt on.

When Chance drove away from the store, she turned to him. "That was totally unnecessary to say nothing of embarrassing. I can buy my own clothes thank you very much." Callie crossed her arms over her chest and looked out the window still seething at the never ending list of questions the shop keeper had thrown at her.

"You are my wife and in my employ. If I want to buy you clothes, I will. Those threadbare jeans might be fine for the heat of the Australian outback, but up here in Montana, they wouldn't keep a gnat warm."

"But I can—"

"Stop arguing is what you can do. Something else you're good at from the sound of things." He mimicked her voice, getting the twang of her voice almost right. "*Only telling it like it is, cowgirl.*"

Callie glared at him, a smile itching the corners of her lips. "Don't make fun of me."

"Well, stop acting like a brat and take the clothing in the

manner it was intended. I don't want you freezing that cute butt of yours off when you're working outside. I need you to take care of yourself as well as me, and I don't think you have any idea of how damned cold it gets here." Chance thumped the steering wheel with his hand and glanced back at her. "Last thing I need is my foreman lost in a snow drift."

Callie scratched behind her ear and looked at him. "Thank you. I appreciate it." She dropped her head. "Who's Jethro?"

He groaned. "Did she give you a hard time about him not getting the job?"

"Kind of."

"He's one of her nephews. Been bad news since his mama died and has given his Grandpa hell. Poor man can't get a decent day's work out of those boys. Hear he's pissed at me for not giving him the job as foreman."

Callie grinned. "Yeah, so is Sue Ellen. I got the third degree over it."

"I'm sorry. I didn't mean for anyone to give you a hard time. I make my own decisions."

"Fair enough." Callie smiled, looked across the seat at him.

"Now that's better. How about you scoot your butt over here and keep me company. We should be home in about ten minutes give or take."

She looked at the distance between them and then unhooked her seat belt, sliding over beside him. Callie pulled on the middle seat belt and settled down to enjoy the final part of their journey, her hand casually resting on her husband's leg.

Chance dropped a hand to her knee and kept it there as they drove through the outskirts of town. The countryside turned denser as the pine forests became thicker. A large boulder marked the road and Callie sat forward when they turned in. The driveway cut through acres of forest before the land became clearer and sunlight filtered through onto the road.

"It's so pretty in here." Any minute now Bambi would come walking out of the forest.

"It is special. Can you blame me for not wanting to go back on the tour?"

Callie shook her head. A shadow hovered in her peripheral vision and she screamed, gripping Chance's thigh.

"Steady on. It's only Brutus. Been here longer than I have." A large moose walked out onto the road and stopped in front of them.

Chance put his foot on the brakes and slowed down to a stop.

"He's huge. Oh, my goodness, that is something."

"He sure is, but don't go thinking he's all cute and fluffy like your kangaroos. He can be as nasty as a bear when he's looking out for his girls. And never ever go near a female with a calf. Nastier than you could imagine."

They sat waiting for Brutus to move on before Chance

put his foot on the gas. The forest quickly faded behind them as cleared paddocks lined either side of the road. The thick green grass took her breath away. "I could get lost in that grass."

Chance pointed to his right. "This bit here is Tyson's spread. It goes all the way up to the bridge ahead. Once you get to the river, the rest all the way up to the mountains is my place."

Callie looked, her mouth dropping open in shock. Ahead of her was a long winding road that snaked up between green pastures to a steep mountain range topped with snow. Around the base of the mountain was another pine forest. "That is so beautiful, just like a postcard."

"Wait until you see the house."

They began the ascent up the hill to the plateau that was Chance's ranch. As they got nearer, Callie could see the roof of a house, chimneys on either side of a large turret topped off with a bell set in the roof. The ground eventually leveled out and the picture of the whole house was in front of them.

"It's a real log home." She stared at the picture-book house with its view over the valley below.

The building had a wide open porch in front that stepped down onto the grass front lawn and tucked around one side. The porch was set out with wooden loungers and side tables to take in the view. Tubs of bright colored flowers broke the starkness of the timber, giving it a homely feel.

Wide French wooden doors led into the main rooms on

either side of the heavy front door. She pointed to the bell up on the roof she'd seen earlier. "What's that for?"

"It's more for decoration than anything. It's an old mission bell I found on my travels. They used to have them at every mission building along the west coast to warn of intruders."

"I like it. Chance, it's just beautiful."

He pulled up beside the house at a wooden hitching rail and let go of her hand. "Come on, let me show you around."

Callie slid across the seat and climbed out, doing a full circle spin to try and take in her surroundings. The property was breathtakingly beautiful. She wouldn't want to leave either if she owned it.

Chance came around and took her hand. "Let's go and have a quick look before it gets dark. I'll give you a guided tour tomorrow." He pulled her toward a large barn on the other side of the driveway. "Stables and covered yards are this way."

She could hear the snorting of horses before he opened the barn door. Along one side of the wall, Callie could make out stalls and the familiar smell the horses reached her nostrils bringing with it a surge of homesickness. Once Chance flicked on overhead lighting she could see where the noises were coming from. The two end stalls were occupied and the animals tossed their heads and whinnied as they approached. He hobbled over and rubbed the nose of the closest horse.

"This here is Sultan and the one next door is Tiny. Neither of them would hurt you, but be careful with Tiny. He has a temper, even with me." The horse not getting the attention hung his head over the door and stamped his feet. Chance moved and held out his hand for him to smell before scratching the forelock. "You can ride Sultan anytime. He's as gentle as a lamb." He checked the horses feed bins. "Looks like Tyson has been up and fed the animals anyway. That'll save us a job tonight and probably a visit from my nosy brother."

Callie reached out a hand and stroked the horse's ears, the heat racing up her cheeks as she thought of the possibilities of a night alone with Chance in his own bed. She turned and looked around the barn. There were stalls on the other side under a mezzanine floor, one that bore a plate with the inhabitant's name. "Where's Pilot?" She walked over and looked in the stable, finding it clean.

"He died last year." The fire burned in his eyes and she took a step back.

"Sorry. I didn't know."

Chance hung his head, breathed deeply before looking back up. The pain in his eyes hurt her. "You couldn't have known. One of the hired hands made him go up a rise they shouldn't have. Too many loose rocks and he lost his footing, broke a leg. They shot him."

"Oh, Chance, that's terrible."

"Yes, it was. He was one of my grandfather's horses. Pilot

was old and shouldn't have been worked at all, he'd earned his retirement. I loved him, plain and simple. He's also one of the reasons I didn't want to get a ranch manager without some sort of stake in the place. I figured if you had more involvement you might take care of things a whole lot better."

"Kind of an extreme measure, don't you think?"

"No, I don't. I have a lot of money tied up here. That horse meant more to me than I can tell you. Apart from that, I can't let anything happen to derail my plans for this place."

"Gee, that makes me feel really wanted. You could have had me here as a manager without marrying me." Being married to keep his stock safer wasn't a bed-warming thought. Damn him for telling her that!

"It didn't suit my plans to not marry you. You're needed here and I don't want you to think otherwise. Pilot was only one of the many reasons I did what I did."

"And the rest of them, why you *really* married me for example?"

"In time, Callie. It's enough that we both get something out of this deal for now."

She bit back a retort knowing he was probably right. If she'd known, she would still have gone along with the deal but it didn't make her feel good. She brushed it off, determined not to let it get to her and concentrated on her inspection of the place. Bales of hay were piled high to the roof for winter feeding, which would last well into spring by the amount stored.

Chance followed her gaze, a look of relief on his face. "We keep a bit of feed in here and there's another feed barn out the back as well as an old worker's cottage that used to be my grandparents' home. Stalls over there"—he pointed to the ones on the opposite wall—"just in case we need to bring in any stock in. Late calves or whatever in the bad weather." A couple of chickens walked out of a stall and stopped to scratch at the floor. "I keep meaning to check in that stall. I bet there's a nest in there full of eggs."

"I'll do it." Callie hurried over and opened the door, scattering the hens. In the far corner she found a nest of eggs. "There must be a couple of dozen here. Fancy eggs for dinner?"

"If you're cooking, I'll have whatever you want to make. Bound to be a basket to collect them somewhere. Let me show you around a bit more and we can come back and get them before we go inside."

Chapter Seven

TOGETHER THEY WALKED out of the barn and turned toward the driveway that ambled away from the house. Paddocks were fenced with picture perfect split posts and whitewashed wooden rails. Cattle grazed lazily and only one bull reared its head to look up as they approached. "This is Terror."

"Terror? You mean the bull that broke your hip?" Callie leaned on the fence and watched the grey and white Brahman amble toward them.

"Yeah, that one. He's a mean old bastard. Don't let that cool, casual look deceive you. He'll turn on you in an instant and because of that, any paddock he's in is out of bounds, understand?" He had to make her see how dangerous Terror was.

She glanced up at him, a wary look in her eyes. "Who gets to manage him then, if I'm not allowed to do it?"

"Tyson can do it until I'm up and able to. I don't care what the issue is, I never want to see you in the same paddock as him. Ever."

"Yes, boss. Geeze, don't get too wound up over it. He's just a damned ornery bull. We have that breed in Australia so I've seen plenty of them in my time."

He grabbed her arm, swinging her around to face him. She still wasn't getting how dangerous the beast was. "Callie, I'm deadly serious here. I've seen him take a man, try and throw him over the railings, and stomp him to death. I don't trust him and neither should you. The only reason he's alive now is because I refused to let them shoot him. I want him for stud and that's all he's good for now. Besides, after what he did to me, I think I deserve him. He's too dangerous to be used as a rodeo bull again."

"Fine. I'll keep out of his way."

Chance ran a hand over his hair, frustration prickling his skin. "I'm sorry. I didn't mean to sound off at you, but I've seen him at his worst. You haven't. It would be easy to be fooled by his nature when he's like this."

"No, that's okay, I understand. Now, what else did you want to show me before it gets too dark out?" She slipped her arm through his.

"Let's take a walk up here further. I had the cows brought down that are calving just to keep an eye on them. Most are a few weeks away, but better to be safe than sorry." Together they walked up driveway where a small herd of cows chewed their grass contentedly, some with calves at foot.

Callie leaned on the fence, her chin on her hands. "This

is all so different to what I'm used to. At home there's more red dirt than grass. The cows have to walk for miles some days to get a decent feed. That's the reason why farmers are going bankrupt so much. No feed unless they truck it in. Been too many years in drought to make farmer a viable option."

Chance rested a hand on her shoulder hating the sadness in her eyes. "We never have that problem here. If anything, I really need to bring in more stock to keep the grass down. We can go to a few sales once you get the hang of the place and you can buy some more."

She looked up at him, interest sparking. "I wouldn't know what to buy. You have so many different cattle here."

"Beef cows are beef cows the world over. Once you get the hang of what breed is what, I'm pretty sure you'll be fine." He shuffled his feet. "Now, I don't know about you, but I could do with heading inside."

"Of course. It's been a long day for you." Callie slung an arm around his waist and led him back to the house. Chance took a key from his pocket and walked up onto the front porch. He slid the key in the lock and pushed the door open, encouraging her to go in before him.

SHE WALKED INSIDE and stopped dead in her tracks. Chance flicked on a light switch and lit up the entryway and lounge to the right of the door. She took a step forward and her jaw dropped. The room was huge with large glass windows that showed off the view of the snow topped mountains and the ranch land sitting at the base of the range. A large black and white mottled cowskin rug lay spread out in front of a wide stone fireplace. It was set ready for a fire with the timber stacked up and plenty of extra logs stacked to one side of the wide hearth. Over the fireplace hung a huge mirror that reflected the view from the front of the house through the large French doors.

She ran her fingers over the leather lounge that was placed back but aimed at the fireplace with a low glass coffee table in front of it. Evenings sitting here wouldn't be a hardship. Bookcases filled the only other internal wall. They were crammed with books and Callie promised herself she would have a look when she had more time.

"This is a stunning room."

"You wait until you see the rest of it." He gripped his cane and told her to follow him. He led her across the hallway into an open plan kitchen. The huge island counter faced the dining table off to one side of the front room with doors that opened onto the porch. Behind the counter, a large six burner gas oven was set into a stone alcove with down lights and an exhaust fan. A double door stainless steel fridge sat beside a door, which Callie assumed was the pantry.

"Have a look around. Open cupboards and do whatever

it is that women do when they check out a house. This is your home now and I want you to be happy here."

"I've never seen anything like this. It's just mind blowing." She walked over to the pantry and opened the door. A light switched on automatically and she stepped inside. The room was almost as large as her bedroom at home. The shelves were laden with food, enough to see them through whatever the weather could throw at them. Chance hobbled up to the door, rested his hand on it.

"Out in the barn is a root cellar, too. Don't know if you know what they are, but basically they're an underground storage room for food. The winters can get really severe here and a lot of the locals like to put down their own food from their gardens to see them through to the next season."

"Do you have a garden?"

"No, not yet. Not really my thing, but if you want one, you just have to say the word."

She gazed at him, amazed at how her life was turning out. "I'd love one. We had a garden of sorts at home, but Mum struggled to grow much because to the lack of water, the heat and the damned rabbits. If she left the covers off the vegetable beds the animals would take everything overnight. Even the crows got really good at taking her vegetables in broad daylight. It was bloody depressing and easier not to bother."

"Just let me know what you want and it'll be done. There are plenty of men in town who know how to build vegetable plots. Landscapers and the like."

"Thanks."

"Let me show you upstairs." He held out his hand and Callie linked her fingers with his. Together they walked from the kitchen to the hallway and started to climb the wide wooden stairs. He pointed past the stairs to the back of the house. "Back there is the laundry, a bathroom, and an office." They continued up the stairs. At the top, Chance paused to rub his hip.

"Our room is the end door. Follow me." He reached for her hand again and led her past several doors on either side of the wide hallway to the master bedroom. Chance opened the door and let her walk in first. She stepped into the room and paused looking at the huge bed. His hand rested on her shoulder and she jumped. "Plenty of room for both of us, but if you like, you can keep your clothes in one of the spare rooms until the brothers come around to my way of thinking." He walked over to the bed and sat down, letting his cane lean against the edge of the mattress. "Shouldn't make much difference to you and me though." He smiled and Callie grinned, her earlier mood gone.

"No, it shouldn't. Are you sure this is how you want to play it? I mean, I could stay in the other room if you like. I wouldn't take offense if you wanted to keep your distance except for the nights you want sex. It's not like this is a conventional marriage and we don't want to blur the lines by getting too cozy."

"I wouldn't be happy with that idea, and it's still a marriage as far as I'm concerned. I want my wife in my bed whenever possible. Come here." He held his arms out and she grinned, keen to get another handful of the naked chest she woke up on this morning. "I know we have a contract but I don't see why we shouldn't enjoy ourselves while we're together."

Callie stood between his legs and put her hands on his shoulders. There was a lot to resolve between them but starving herself of enjoyment while she sorted that out wasn't really on her list. The year would be over before she knew it and Australia would be calling. She dipped her head and placed her mouth on his. Gently at first they kissed, reigniting the bond that was quickly building up between them.

His arms came around her back, lowering to cup her butt and pull her closer. Callie pushed herself against him suddenly desperate for more. Moving her hips against him, the heat built in her body.

She moaned as he pulled her shirt from her jeans. His fingers reached up to undo her buttons and she shrugged it from her shoulders to drop on the floor. Chance's roughened hands circled her waist, his breath hot against her stomach. She gasped as he dipped his tongue into her belly button while he popped the button on her pants. Callie helped him push her jeans down and stepped out of them, kicking them away. He gripped her butt in his hands and lifted her to her tiptoes.

Callie cried out as he ran his tongue over the front of her panties, hinting of what was to come. His fingers dug under the elastic and suddenly she stood before him naked and wanting.

"You're so beautiful." The wonder in his voice made her brave and she pulled him to his feet. With trembling hands, Callie undid the buttons on his shirt and pushed it apart to shower his chest with her lips. His fingers toyed with her nipples as she worked her way down to the button on his jeans. He helped her to shuck them down to his ankles and stepped out of them, kicking them out of the way.

"This might be better on the bed." Chance pulled down the covers and guided her onto the soft mattress. He leaned over her, gazing at her nakedness, a smile on his face.

She blushed under his scrutiny, wishing he would hurry up and take her. She was desperate for her hot cowboy. Watching his erection twitching against his stomach was almost more than she could stand. Callie reached out and wrapped her hand around it, her thumb rubbing over the head.

"I doubt I'll last long if you do that." He gasped and closed his eyes, breathing hard.

"Well then, perhaps we should just get on with it. We can play around a bit more next time."

"Since you put it that way, I'd have to agree." He kissed her, dipping his tongue into her mouth as he lowered himself between her legs. His fingers trailed down her belly into the small patch of hair crowning the apex of her thighs. Chance slid his fingers between her lips and Callie squirmed in pleasure. She was wet and ready for him and doubted she'd last very long if he toyed with her like that.

"Now, Chance. Please don't tease me. I need you inside me right now." She pushed her hips against his, eager for him to fill her.

When he slid inside her, Callie gasped and moaned loudly, her hands grasping his naked butt.

"Did I hurt you?" Chance stilled his body.

She wrapped her legs around his thighs, careful with his sore hip and thrust herself against him. "No." She ground out. "Hard and fast, now."

Chance did as she asked, pushing her toward an earth-shattering orgasm within minutes. Callie cried out as she fell over the edge, her fingers digging into his butt, holding him in place as her sex quivered around him. With a final deep thrust, Chance went over and joined her.

Chapter Eight

CHANCE OPENED HIS eyes in the morning with Callie tucked into his shoulder. Her lips moved with each outward breath and soft snore. It was cute and he smiled, wondering how annoyed she'd be if he mentioned it. It seemed as though she had the best sleep last night and after the last few days he wasn't surprised. Moving halfway across the world to meet the future husband she had to have to save the family name from creditors would be tough on anyone. To find out they were compatible was a huge bonus, but Chance had thought they might've been anyway. Even in her photo, she had an attitude that screamed independent and strong. Just what he needed after years of being fawned over by ditzy women who were more interested in being the wife of a famous bull rider and entrepreneur than a rancher who wanted to work hard and make his breeding program a success.

A smile crossed his lips as he tried and failed to imagine Libby Tucker working in the yards, feeding the animals or cleaning out stables shoveling horse poo. The wanna-be famous actress had decided early on to attach her star to Chance's, letting drop more than once that if she had the money behind her, she'd be more successful. Every possible opportunity for a photo draped over his arm, she took it and Chance knew most of the tip-offs came from her.

When he had downtime, she always seemed to be staying at the same hotel and more than once had managed to get into his room and his bed. Not saying she hadn't been fun to hang out with, but the thought of spending his life with her left a sour taste in his mouth. She wasn't someone he wanted to bring home to the ranch no matter how much Tyson thought they looked great together.

Unlike the woman sleeping soundly in his arms right at this minute. The moment Chance had seen the photograph of Callie and heard her down-to-earth voice, he'd known she was the one who could help him out of his predicament. Spending the next year with her wouldn't be hard. He hoped her desire for money would be enough for her to agree to anything he suggested and she had. When they skyped, he'd listened to her voice and let the Australian twang roll over his body. She knew what she was talking about when it came to ranching, or farming as she called it. Her no-nonsense approach had won him over instantly. Here was a woman he could see himself growing old with. One who he hoped would stick with him through the rough patches as well as the good. He just had to make sure she was happy here and wanted to stay with him after their contract ran out. He had until then to figure out if she really was the one for him and not a mistake like the ones in the past. Chance wasn't prepared to go through that again.

The first bout of married sex had probably helped to settle Callie into a good sleep, too. It had certainly worked for him. Thinking about it made his body tense up, ready for more of the same. It was only the pain in his hip when he moved toward her that made him rethink that idea. A hot shower and some painkillers were probably a better plan. He couldn't wait until he had the pins out. Then the muscles would heal and he would get better movement.

Callie's nose twitched and she reached up to brush her hand over it. When she touched his chest she opened her eyes and for a moment looked lost and startled.

"Hey." He leaned in and kissed the tip of her nose and watched the color fill her cheeks, highlighting the small scattering of freckles across her cheeks that he hadn't noticed curled right around to her ears before.

"Hey, yourself." A smile broke out on her face and she rested her hand on his chest, her fingers warm and light against his skin. "How are you feeling this morning?"

"Horny as all hell, but I think I'd be better with some drugs and a hot shower. As much as I'd like to say more of last night's action would appeal to me, I doubt I'd be able to do much on the ranch today if I make love to you again."

"Such a shame. I was looking forward to wake-up sex." She pouted and ran her tongue across his lips, teasing and taunting him.

When he lunged for her mouth she pulled back and laughed.

"Stick to the plan, cowboy. You have to show me what to do. Not going to be any good if you can't get your butt out of bed." She threw the blankets from their bodies and uncurled herself from against him. Rising from the bed, Callie looked at him as she slid away to stand on the floor.

He watched as she turned away and walked naked to the bathroom, her hips swaying with each step, teasing his already rampant libido just a little bit more. She wound her hair up into a knot on the top of her head securing with an elastic band from the dresser as she passed it and disappeared from his sight. Chance lay back thinking of how lucky he'd been picking her for his wife. His brothers were going to be hard to convince, but it was what he wanted that counted.

Having to break it to the hordes of fans around the country was going to be harder but they'd attach their dedication to the next rising star soon enough. His manager had left it up to Chance to break the news after he'd told his family. Chance received mail every day from people who couldn't wait for him to come back from his accident and eagerly waited for the next bull ride so they could come along and support him. The offers of help had poured in. Even offers of private nurses should he need them. He knew what that meant. Women who wanted him in bed at their mercy, no nursing included. But he was sick of that life and wanted the plain and simple joy of working the land and the animals.

The sound of water running in the shower reached him and he decided a romp under the hot water could work for him. Sex and heat on his sore hip might just be the best way to start his day. He rolled out of bed and used his hand on the wall to help support him as he shuffled along to the bathroom. The steam rose from the large open tile shower and Callie stood with her back to him, the water running in channels down her naked back. Chance held onto the wall and stepped under the hot water, sliding one arm around her waist and leaning into her back, his cock standing proud against her butt cheeks.

"Took you long enough. I'd almost given up waiting for you." Callie turned around and grabbed his face in her hands, planting her lips against his. "I promise I'll be gentle with you."

"Don't hold back on my account." Chance held his breath as she grinned and slid down his body to kneel in front of him. He tilted his head back and let the water stream over his face while his wife gave him the best head job he'd ever had.

"SEX MAKES ME hungry. What can I say?"

Callie scooped another ladle of scrambled eggs onto her

plate. "I must remember to collect those eggs today. You distracted me yesterday with other things. There aren't any more in the fridge." She sat at the table, looking out the doors over the porch eating her breakfast when a truck came up the driveway.

"Shit. Might of known he wouldn't take long to come and stick his nose in." Chance groaned. "Sorry, it's Tyson. Let's see how this goes then, shall we. Don't let him boss you around. Remember you're the new ranch manager."

She swallowed the irritation that crawled up her throat. Ranch manager, not wife. It stung even though it shouldn't have. Why Chance couldn't come out and say it up front annoyed her but it was his gig. He was the one wielding the checkbook so she had no say in it. *I can do this, I can do this.* Callie ate her second helping of eggs as she waited for her new secret brother-in-law to come in and give her the third degree. She didn't have to wait long.

The door opened and a man who looked very much like a younger version of Chance walked in the door, his hat in his hand. "Chance." He nodded at Callie. "Morning. Who's this?"

"Callie, meet Tyson, my very nosy brother. Tyson, I want you to meet Callie, my new ranch manager.

"What? Are you fucking kidding me? A woman?"

She shrank back in her chair, unprepared for the venom he was dishing out.

"Watch your mouth. She's more than capable of running

this place so back off." Chance stood up, grabbing his cane from beside the chair as he rose.

"I don't believe this. You not only get a ranch manager from damned Australia of all places instead of employing Jethro, but it's a bloody female."

"And you will honor my decision and treat her with the respect you would treat a sister if you were lucky enough to have one, understand?" Chance walked over to him and poked him in the chest.

Tyson looked past Chance at Callie and his gaze hardened. "You have no idea what you've done here, brother. You're getting ripped off because of who you are and the money you make. You mark my words."

"I told you to back off, Tyson. I won't have you disrespecting anyone in my home."

Callie stood up and reached for her new hat. "Don't worry about him, Chance. Stands to reason people are going to talk about me when they know nothing about me and what I'm capable of. I can take it." She jammed the hat on her head and brushed past the men and headed outside to the barn.

Chapter Nine

C HANCE WATCHED HER go, his blood on the boil.
"How the hell do you think someone like that is
going to manage this place when you're back on the tour?
She'll get blown away in the first snow drift, then what'll you
do?"

Chance turned on his brother. "Give her a decent go before you judge her. The girl has been running the family
station in Australia since she was a kid. Apart from the fact
their cattle breeds are slightly different and the seasons are
around the wrong way, she has it all under control."

"Yeah right, I'll believe that when I see it." He walked
past his brother and over to the kitchen island to grab
himself a cup of coffee. "I spoke to Rory yesterday. Trying to
talk him into coming for a visit. He said he'd think about it."

The change of subject threw Chance off for a second.
"What? Oh right. Well I guess it's time he came out of his
shell. It's been three years." He listened with one ear, but was
more concerned about what his wife was doing outside.

Tyson walked over sipping the dark hot brew. "So, when

do you go back to the doctors?"

"Three weeks."

"Want me to take you?" Tyson watched him over his mug of coffee.

"Nope. Callie can drive me there and back. May as well make the most of having someone around the place. There is something you can do for me though. I was thinking of getting a dog to keep her company since the place will have someone living here permanently now. Know anyone local who has one available?"

"Yeah. Old Jim Puller has a litter of cattle cross dogs. Might be worth a look at. But don't you think you ought to wait and see if she turns out? She could be gone in a week you know, and then you'll have to find a new home for it." He put his coffee down and leaned on the counter with both hands. "You know I can always help out. I keep telling you that."

"Look, Tyson, I appreciate that but you need to concentrate on your own place. You've done enough for me over the years. It's time I looked after my own ranch."

"Bit hard when you're away so much. Let's see how wonder girl works out. Bet she doesn't last any longer than the others."

"We'll see. Don't go spouting off at her anymore either and she might just surprise you. Now, if there's nothing else you want, I'm going to go and show her what her job entails." He grabbed his hat and cane and hobbled toward the door. "How's the horse trade going anyway?"

Tyson left his coffee mug on the kitchen counter and followed. "Picked up another contract to supply broncos to one of the big rodeos. Just have to go and find some more brood mares that are within my budget. I reckon if I can find another dozen, I should be able to keep up supply pretty easy."

"I can give you some more cash." Chance held the door for his brother.

"No way. You've done more than any brother should do. Helped me buy the place next door and set it up. I can manage fine. Put your money away for a rainy day. Heck, in another ten years or so you'll be too damned old to ride bulls and need the money for yourself and that high maintenance bride you'll probably bring home."

"Is that what you think I'm going to do; bring home a damned starlet or something?"

"Sure, why not? You've always got one on your arm, stands to reason you'd marry one. Seriously." Tyson scoffed and pointed down the drive to where Callie was tipping a barrow full of horse poo onto the heap outside the barn. "Can you imagine being married to someone like her? I mean, she's so not your type, brother."

She is exactly my type. You just have no idea who I really am and what's good for me. Yet. "Never say never. Now, gotta go. Thanks for helping out with the animals while I was away. I'll catch you later." Chance waved to his brother and walked as fast as his hip would let him toward the barn, listening as Tyson's truck started up and rolled off down the driveway.

He hurried inside the barn using his cane to regulate his steps. "Sorry about that." He leaned on the railing and watched as Callie put clean hay in the horse's feed troughs. She'd opened the door to let them out and they were busy grazing in the paddock.

"No problem. Not your fault he has no idea what's going on. Can't say I like his attitude though. Chauvinistic bastard." She threw down the shavings for bedding and stomped back to pick up the pitchfork, using it to level the floor of the stall evenly.

"Yeah, well, that's probably my fault really. He's not really had a woman in his life for quite some time, and our father wasn't exactly the best teacher he could have had."

"Still doesn't account for bad manners." She looked up at him, eyes clouded with disappointment.

Chance reached out and pulled her to his chest. "I'm sorry, baby, you didn't deserve that. I feel bad we have to do it this way, but it's for the best in the long run."

"Yeah, I suppose. I should just let it go but it kind of hurt, you know?"

He tipped her face up and kissed her soundly. Callie melted against him and Chance could think of nothing more appealing than pushing her back onto the clean hay and taking her once again. He would never be able to get enough of this woman. Once his brothers realized how wonderful he felt with her around, they would see reason. They had to.

"This isn't getting the jobs done." She smiled and slapped him playfully on the butt before stepping out of his arms.

"True. I was hoping you could go around the cows and see how they're going. Let me know if there are any calves and if they need anything."

"Sure. Can I take the horse?"

"Yep. Let me show you how to call him in."

CHANCE LIFTED HIS fingers to his lips and whistled long and low. Sultan lifted his head and looked at them before taking a step toward the barn. "Saddles are over there in the tack room. Take whichever one you want. I normally use the western on him but you might not be used to one of those."

"I'll have you know I rode in one once and really liked it. They're a bit more solid than what we use back home and I can deal with it." Callie walked toward the tack room and pushed open the door. A row of saddles sat on a beam that took up one entire wall. She walked over and ran her hands over a pale golden saddle, tooled with rose patterns over the fender right around to the skirt. The seat of the saddle was made of suede in the same honey color as the rest of the saddle. Even the stirrups and the cinch strap were decorated.

"This is just beautiful." Callie ran her fingers over the intricate carvings and decided this was the one she wanted to ride in today. She heaved it up in her arms and carried it out to the stall where Sultan now stood having a head rub with Chance. "This is one gorgeous saddle. Are you sure it's okay if I use it?" She hoisted it over the gate.

"Of course it is. I told you to choose whichever one you wanted. This one I won a long time ago and it's never been used. Consider it yours. Now, you'd better go and get a saddle blanket and a bridle for him. Make it a soft one because you don't need to be on his mouth at all. Sultan works better when you use your legs to guide him."

Callie hurried back to the tack room and looked for a suitable bridle and chose a woven blanket for under the saddle. When she got back, Chance had brought Sultan out of the stall and he was standing waiting to go to work.

"This guy is very calm normally, but he hasn't been ridden for a while so don't be surprised if he leads the way. He knows what to do and you won't come to any harm with him. Knows the place better than I do, I reckon."

"Sounds good, thanks." Callie saddled the horse, excitement building in her chest.

To get back on a horse again was going to be invigorating. For too long, she'd been without an animal to ride and to go out in the paddocks and check on the cows and calves was something she was dying to do. How hard could it be to check out the progress of the next four-hoofed generation?

Once she had the cinch strap tight enough, she held the bridle up to Sultan's head. He opened his mouth and accepted the bit between his teeth, all the time rubbing his head against Chance's outstretched hand.

"He's such a softie." Chance waited until she was ready to mount and handed her his jacket. "You'll need this. It gets pretty cold out there. You might not think so right now, but the wind can come down off that mountain and cut through you like a knife. A pair of gloves wouldn't hurt either next time."

Callie slid her arms into the sheepskin lined jacket and instantly felt the difference. "Thanks." She placed her foot in the stirrup and pulled herself up, holding onto the pommel of the saddle. Once her leg was across the horse's back, she settled herself down on the comfortable seat, wiggling her butt to make sure it was right for her. Chance shortened her stirrups and then she was ready to go.

"Don't take any chances out there with your safety, okay? I don't think there'll be anything to worry about, but the weather can turn at any time. You need to keep an eye on the sky because I won't be able to come looking for you until I have better use of my hip."

"Don't fuss, I'll be fine. Checking on stock is something I used to do all the time. You go inside and rest that hip. It's going to get another workout tonight if I have my way." She winked at him and used her knees to push Sultan out of the barn and headed to do her job.

The first paddock housed the famous Terror and she glanced him over as she passed by. He was a good-looking Brahman; there was no doubt about it. Didn't look like he had a mean bone in his body but after what he'd done to Chance, she would keep an eye on him. In the paddock with him were a large group of yearlings. They were all young bulls, and she guessed these guys were destined for the rodeo arena if they played up as well as Terror did.

She ambled past them and cast her eye over the opposite paddock where fat Angus cows grazed lazily in the morning sun. A couple seemed to have calved already and Callie wondered just how large these paddocks were. She would find out soon enough.

At the gate, she leaned down and unhitched the catch, pushing with her foot to give the horse enough room to pass through before locking it behind her. The grass was long and brushed up past the horse's hocks. Rich, tall grass that could hide a small calf if she wasn't watching for it carefully.

Callie decided to ride the fence first to make sure there were no breaks and that way she would get an idea of the size of paddock she was dealing with. She rode for hours, criss-crossing the area so she could find all the stock to check on them. A couple of the mothers charged at Sultan if they got too close in a show of bravado but, overall, the day was calm and easy. Being back in the saddle gave her a sense of pride in the job she was doing, which she loved. Whatever the outcome, Callie would give this contract her best shot because that was how she was brought up.

It wasn't until after lunch that her stomach started to rumble and she decided to go in for a feed. These girls would have to be watched carefully for the next couple of weeks to make sure there were no cows struggling with the birth process. Even losing one calf was a hit to any farmer. Losing its mother as well could be devastating and there was the breeding program to think of. Chance wanted it improved, not downgraded and she wanted her bonus.

She was unsaddling Sultan when she heard Chance coming toward her.

"Where the hell have you been? I've been worried sick."

Chapter Ten

CHANCE NOTICED THE way her back stiffened and could have kicked himself for his choice of words and the tone he'd used. "I'm sorry. I didn't mean to snap at you. I was worried when it took you so long."

She undid the cinch strap before she pulled the saddle from Sultan's back. Without looking at Chance, Callie lugged it to the door of the stall and threw it across the wooden rail. When she turned back to him, her face was set and angry. "You hired me to do a job, deal with it." Callie grabbed a brush and gave the horse a quick rubdown before letting him walk into the stall.

"I said I was sorry. I know you have a job to do and I understand that, but it's your first day out there and I was worried, okay?" How could he tell her his true feelings when he didn't know them himself. All he could think of while she was out was that he wanted her back with him.

She reached up and kissed his cheek, following it with the palm of her hand, cupping him with a gentle slap. "Try not to be a smothering husband. There's a good boy."

Callie grabbed her saddle and took it to the tack room, leaving him wondering what he'd taken on. She was more independent than he had thought she would be and he rather liked it.

"Have you looked at the sky lately?"

"Nope. It wasn't raining so I didn't think it was a problem." She came out of the tack room with a bucket and headed to the corner of the barn where the chickens had been hiding their eggs. She reached down and scooped them up into the bucket and then waltzed back to him. "I could go for a coffee and something to eat before I do the afternoon chores."

Chance let his angst ease away knowing he was being irrational and overprotective with his new bride. "What can I get you for lunch? Seems the least I can do since you are doing all the outside work while I can't."

"Well, now, that depends on what you're offering, cowboy." She winked at him and Chance's blood pounded faster through his veins.

"You're going to be the death of me at this rate, woman. I can just imagine what the doctor is going to say when I go back to get the pins out. 'Not healing, Mr. Watson. What have you been doing? Not resting that hip as I suggested by the look of things.'"

Callie laughed and slapped her hand on her leg. "You started it, pal. I was quite happy to ease into the whole sex thing, getting to know you slowly because the ranch was the key thing here, but you just had to take it fast. You have nobody to blame but yourself."

"And I wouldn't have it any other way. After lunch I want to take you into town to look at some pups. Now we're going to be living here full time I think a dog is doable. What do you say?"

The light in her eyes said it all. "Really? I miss my dogs. I had to shoot them before I left." A shudder raced over her skin and Chance grabbed her arm.

"Why couldn't you re-home them?" He hated to see the pain in her eyes as she talked about the dogs.

"Because there are too many stations that're struggling to feed the stock they have. Another couple of farm dogs rate very low on the scale of importance when you live in the outback where everyone is fighting to make ends meet."

"I'm sorry. But talking of guns, I must show you the gun locker in case you need a weapon for anything—an emergency or a cougar attack."

"Cougars, you get them out here?" Her eyes widened and he watched the flicker of color change around her iris.

"Rarely, but yes, sometimes. I haven't had one here since I've owned the place, but it pays to be prepared anyway. I know of two deaths in the last ten years in the mountains close by. Not keen to make that three if we can help it." He placed an arm around her shoulders. "Let's get you fed and we can go into town and choose a pup."

Chance made her sit down and put her feet up while he

prepared a steak sandwich and a large coffee.

When he placed it in front of her, Callie picked it up with both hands and smiled. "Are you trying to fatten me up?"

"No. I figure you need decent fuel if you're going to be working hard and you can't do that on an empty stomach. Eat up, it's good, even if I say so myself."

He watched as she took a big bite, the juice from the home grown meat dribbling down her chin. With a laugh she wiped it away with the back of her hand before he could suggest doing it for her. Was he so easy to read where she was concerned?

"WE'RE GOING TO have to make some rules." She saw the desire that sparked in his eyes when she took the first bite of her lunch.

"Oh, really. And they would be what?" He looked at her with an innocent expression on his face but she could see through him.

"No sex during the working day." As she said the words, she mentally kicked herself. Never before had she had sex in a hayloft and, seeing as there was one on the ranch, she was having all kinds of fantasies about using it to its full potential.

"You don't really mean that, do you?" He looked so

crestfallen she had to grin.

"I do. At least I think I do. For now anyways, at least until I get the hang of this place and everything is sorted with your brothers." She took another bite and chewed while thinking. "It wouldn't look good if they arrived unannounced and caught us in the act when they don't even know we're married. Tyson would think he was on the right track about me being after your money."

"Might save some explaining later on."

"Somehow I doubt that and I don't want to be in the line of his nasty mouth again. Pretty sure it would make things more awkward for everyone. No, we need to stick to the original plan and let them get to know me and see how happy you are here on the ranch before we break it to them."

She watched the emotions in her husband's eyes as he warred with himself over her words.

"I want to test out every possible place we can have sex once my hip is better. That's a promise and that's how long I'm going to give my brothers to get used to you before we come clean and tell them the truth."

"I can live with that. I'll keep you to it, too. I often wondered what it would be like to wake up with hay in my hair." She laughed at the face he pulled. "I never said I was a prude or frigid. Stop looking at me that way. Sex is normal."

"I couldn't agree more. I just never expected to find someone who would be as easy to get on with as you are." He looked at her with a strange look in his eyes and she faltered.

"You mean easy in bed, don't you?" She put her sandwich down on the plate and picked up the napkin to dab at her mouth.

Maybe she'd gone too far, given in too early. *You idiot, Callie.* She wouldn't get a chance like this again and here she might have already blown it.

"No, I don't and I wish you didn't have such a low opinion of yourself. When we skyped I knew you had a determined attitude and I like that about you. I had hoped we would be sexually compatible because that always helps in my opinion. It would be terrible to live with someone who didn't turn you on without trying. You do that for me and I hope it goes both ways. That doesn't make you easy or slutty, if that's what you're thinking. It makes us both very lucky to have found one another."

Callie looked at him, hoping he was telling her what he firmly believed and not what she wanted to hear.

"If it wasn't for the risk of someone knocking on the door now, I'd take you on this table and damn the consequences. That is what you do to me, Callie. Thinking about it makes me as horny as hell." He wiped a hand across his forehead in dramatic fashion.

She laughed, the sound filling the large open plan room. "Well, since you said it so nicely, how can I not believe you? I'm sorry, I don't mean to be so touchy but I'm pretty sure someone else will come up with something along those lines."

"Not if I have anything to do with it, believe me. My brothers I can deal with. Anyone else has no business making assumptions when they know nothing about us. Now, eat up and let's go and find you a new dog."

When they pulled up at the home where Tyson said there were pups for sale, Callie got excited. It'd broken her heart to put her dogs down but there was no other option. It would have been cruel to leave them on the farm when there was nobody coming in to take over and work the place. She'd take what was offered and not think about saying goodbye when the time came. At least she knew Chance would be there to look after it and she wouldn't have to take out the gun.

She jumped from the truck and waited for Chance to get out. The excited barking of puppies rose over the shouts of a man trying his best to gain control. Together, Chance and Callie walked toward the gate and looked over the fence of the cottage set on the front of a small holding. The tin barrier held in a litter of boisterous pups fighting over an old man's boots as they tried to pin him down and he struggled to get away. "Get down. Go on, get." He waved his arms at them to no avail. They were determined to latch onto his boots and use them for a chew toy.

"Looks like they've got you surrounded, Jim." Chance leaned on the fence and laughed as the old man tried to step away from the pups.

"Chance? Heard tell you were at the ranch recuperating. Give me a hand here will you, young lady. Damned pups have taken a shine to my boots and I can't seem to get away from them." He waved his hands to brush them away but, being as frail as he was, he was no match for the fast growing litter.

Callie hopped over the fence and walked into the melee, picked up a couple of pups and tucked them under her arms. She backed off and the others followed her leaving the old man time to get out of the dogs' yard. He hurried over to Chance and she was left holding the wriggling bundles of fluff.

"Well aren't you just the cutest little creatures." The two pups decided she was the next toy to play with and gleefully licked at her chin, wriggling to get closer, their sharp little teeth nipping at her skin. She squealed and laughed as she made her way to the fence, suddenly the center of attention.

Chance watched her, something in his eyes she couldn't make out. Was it passion or was he thinking of something more? He was such an open person some time and then his mood changed and she couldn't read him at all.

"Thanks, little lady. They're getting to the handful stage. Don't know why I even bother breeding them anymore. About time I stopped and let someone else do the dirty work."

"Come on now, Jim. You always have great dogs. These ones look top class."

"Yeah, I know, but I'm getting too damned long in the tooth for this mucking around. This might be my last litter. Now, who is this pretty lady you have here with the cute accent?"

"Callie, I want you to meet Jim. Known him since I was knee high. Jim, Callie moved over from Australia to be my ranch manager."

"Australia you say. Now that's a fair long distance to come for a job, missy."

"Yeah, I guess, but it was advertised and just what I wanted so I thought, why not. You know what they say, a change is as good as a holiday."

He eyed her up and down, obviously giving her answer some consideration. "Hmmm, guess I can't argue with that then." He turned back to Chance. "So what are you doing here? After a dog at long last?"

"Thought it might be high time I got one. Now Callie is living on the ranch I think it might be a good idea. A cattle dog that can act as a companion would be handy."

Jim chewed it over and looked between the two of them. "Right. Well, you can choose a pup if you like. None of them are taken just yet, but I doubt they will last long once I put the word out. You prepared to train the little rascal, missy?" He pinned his dark little eyes on Callie and she blushed under his scrutiny.

"Done it before, and I'm pretty sure I can do it again."

"Callie comes off a station in Australia, Jim. Had her

own dogs over there." She knew Chance was trying to make things easier for her with the old man. He'd told her on the way down Jim had a reputation for being a hard hitter and not to take anything he said personally.

"Girl can talk for herself, can't she?"

"Of course I can. I'm not a fool. What did you want to know?" Callie waited for him to take her to task as Tyson had.

"What do you know about the breed?" He leaned on the fence and watched her carefully.

"Australian cattle dog. Clever, fast, and deadly loyal. I had two I had to destroy when I left because our station was taken by the bank and nobody wanted them."

"Damned shame that. So, you prepared to take on a pup, scattered as they are?"

A grey and white cattle dog jumped the fence and sidled its way up to Callie, sniffing her boots before sitting down beside her. The dog had one blue eye and one brown eye, a trait that popped up every now and then but didn't affect the dog's ability to see what it was doing.

"Sherbet, get outta there. Go on, get." Jim waved his hands at the dog, but it turned its head and ignored him.

"Damn stupid thing. Lost her pups and been acting silly ever since."

Callie glanced at Chance before putting down the pups. "How old is she?"

"Hmm, about four years old, I reckon. First litter was

good, second not so great, and the last one a total failure. Not much good for breeding, which is good, 'cause I've just about had enough."

Callie reached down and stroked the dog's ears. It looked up at her with its odd colored eyes and leaned into her leg.

"How much for her, Jim?" Chance winked at Callie and she smiled, surprised he was on the same wavelength as her.

"You want her? She's yours, Chance. Can't sell her as a breeder and I doubt anyone with a lick of sense would want her over a good pup."

"Woo-hoo." Callie ran back in the fenced yard and whistled to the dog, holding her arm in the air.

Sherbet turned and ran, sailing over Callie's arm with ease, following her every move with intense concentration. Callie crouched and flicked her fingers and the dog launched over her back spinning on her feet to await the next command. The whistle for "way back" sounded and the dog flew over the fence.

Callie signaled her back and held her arms out, waiting for the ball of energy to soar into her embrace.

"Looks like you have yourself a dog, Callie." Chance grinned as she stood amongst the pups with the cattle dog in her arms.

Sherbet licked at her face and Callie laughed with delight before putting her down on the ground. She held out her hand to the old man. "Thanks so much, Jim. She's just perfect for what I want." She lifted her leg and scooted over the fence and Sherbet followed, sticking close to her new owner.

"Damnedest thing, ain't it? They always say a dog chooses it owner. Guessing she finally found hers." Jim scratched his head and grinned. "Glad to see her going to a good home, too. Don't know what I would have done with her otherwise."

"Oh, she'll be looked after. I can assure you of that."

Together, the three of them walked back to the truck and Sherbet jumped in as soon as the door opened and nestled on the floor beside Callie's feet, signaling her position in the family. Jim followed, leaned on the door of the truck. "Looking like we might get a drift of snow the next couple of days." He rubbed his lower back. "Damn winter storms are making me ache all over."

"But it's almost spring, isn't it? At least I thought it was. Don't think I've mixed up the seasons and it's nearly autumn at home."

"Yep, you got it right. Can't make head nor tail of the weather some days."

Callie looked at the old man and then up at the sky. "How can you tell?"

"Haven't you seen the blackbirds flying around? Always a sign of snow when they take to the sky in droves and circling overhead like they have been last couple of days. Right pretty red sunsets, too. Anytime this week coming I reckon, you mark my words."

Chapter Eleven

SHERBET FOLLOWED CALLIE around the rest of the afternoon, dogging her every step. Chance let her go and do her jobs and, since his hip was hurting, he sat on the front porch and relaxed. His stress levels were low for the first time in weeks. He loved being home at the ranch and having Callie here was the best thing that could have happened to him. It was a shame he had to have her here under false pretenses as far as his brothers were concerned, but he was sure they'd all come around sooner or later. He hoped for sooner so he could come out about his future and then all he had to do was work on Callie once he'd decided for sure she was the one.

After Tyson's visit this morning, he'd decided it was time he called Rory and pushed him to come and visit. He missed his brother. There had to be something he could do for him to bring him back into the fold. He picked up the phone and dialed the number.

"Denver Sheriff, Deputy Watson speaking."

"Rory, it's Chance."

"Chance, well what do you know. The famous one is calling me. What's happened, brother, run out of rich people to spend your time with?" The bitterness in his voice was a shock. They'd been close as teenagers until Chance had run, leaving Rory to hold the fort with the other boys and their drunken father.

"Since when has that been an issue between us? I wanted to see how you were doing?"

"One day after another, same as always." A deep sigh sounded over the phone. "Sorry, I don't mean to take it out on you. Some days are great, some suck like you wouldn't believe."

"Rory, you can always take it out on me. What do you think family's for?" He missed the closeness they used to share. "When are you coming home? It's about time, don't you think?"

"I just don't know what to do anymore. I thought if I stayed here I'd get over Cindy and it would be enough, but it isn't."

Chance could hear the weariness in his brother's voice. "Put in for a transfer or just throw it all in. Come and stay with me for a while until you know what you want to do. Buy a ranch of your own if you want or work in town. Pretty sure there're enough offences happening in a town the size of Marietta to warrant you moving back home." Chance looked over the view and his gaze was drawn to beyond the forest deep in the valley where the town was nestled just out of sight. He'd love Rory to be so close again.

"I already gave notice and applied in Marietta for a job. Decided it was time. I'm just waiting to hear if I got it or not."

A spark of hope settled in Chance's chest. To have his brothers all back in town would be the ultimate buzz. "It will happen, just you wait and see. You can stay with me. I have heaps of room as you know."

"From what I understand, you have a new housemate already. Not sure I want to cramp your style."

"Tyson." His little brother was the town gossip. Chance was convinced of it.

"Yep, that one never could keep anything to himself. Besides, with you going back on the tour, your new manager might want the place to herself. I can get accommodation in town anyways. Maybe catch up with the old man and see what he's been up to."

At the mention of their father, Chance grimaced. "Can't see how he'd change. Once a drunk always a drunk."

"Let's agree to disagree, shall we? You weren't there to see everything so don't go judging him like that."

Chance heard the words and took the hit to the gut, knowing Rory was right. Still, he doubted his father had changed any since Chance had left home. Sitting at the kitchen table with a bottle of whiskey for company while the boys brought themselves up was a poor excuse for a father. And when he lost it, they all suffered. Until the day Chance up and left.

"Right. What he does no longer concerns me." He rubbed his knuckles over the faded patch in his jeans and looked over the ranch. The chill was more noticeable now than it was yesterday. Snow for sure. "So, have you heard from Evan lately?"

"Nope, not for a bit now. Last time I heard he was still in Dallas at the hospital."

"Yeah, me, too. Well, you take care and let me know when you get that transfer. Can't wait to see you, Rory. It's been too damn long."

"Likewise. Gotta run." The phone disconnected and Chance put it on the table beside him. He lazed in the chair and waited for Callie to come back. He missed her already.

ONCE THE HORSES had been brought in and the chickens fed, Callie walked over to the fence and gazed at the cows, marveled at the calves busy suckling. Sherbet sat beside her and leaned into her leg. Callie reached down and rubbed the ears of her new best friend, thankful Chance had taken her down to visit Jim when he had. A dog completed her in a way she couldn't explain. On the farm, the dogs had been like an extra pair of hands and here on the ranch Sherbet would save her a lot of work. She was a well-trained cattle dog and the two of them had bonded immediately. She also filled up the hole in her heart that stood empty the moment she'd pulled the trigger.

The dog moved her head and growled low in her throat. When Callie turned it was to see Terror at the fence, pawing at the ground, his head down in a show of aggression that would have been frightening if Callie was on the other side of the fence. "Give it up, big guy, you don't scare me. Seen tougher than you in the desert where I used to live."

The bull snorted and tossed his head around, intent on intimidating her. She ignored him, turned, and glanced over the cow paddock again, looking for any sign of trouble. Seeing none, she snapped her fingers and Sherbet followed her back down the driveway to the house. Chance sat on the front porch, gazing silently over the valley.

"Hey." She dropped down into a chair beside him.

He glanced at her, gave a smile, and reached for her hand. "Hey, everything okay?"

"Yes. Why do I think it's the calm before the storm though? The ranch seems bathed in a kind of eerie light." She looked up at the mountains but couldn't shake the weird tingling up her spine. Callie stared at the hazy cast over the mountains, unsettled by the unfamiliar sight.

"Snow coming. Jim was right, look at the birds overhead."

She raised her eyes to the sky and watched as the birds circled the house, high enough that they were silently gliding on the wind overhead. "Hmm, best I get out there early in the morning then and make sure the cows are okay. Any idea how long it's likely to last?"

"Depends on how much we get. Might only be a light dusting although I doubt it. We could be snowed in for a week or so. Damned inconvenient time for a flash storm with calves arriving."

She grinned. "I can make a snowman. It's going to be so exciting seeing snow for the first time." Callie and her sisters had yearned for a trip to the ski fields but it was never in the family budget so she had yet to touch the cold, white powder and she was excited about the prospect. "Or snow angels. Now that would be awesome."

"I don't want you putting yourself in harm's way, understand? I can't come and rescue you if you run into trouble. You need to be careful out there and not take unnecessary chances."

"I know how to handle myself. Don't fuss. Now, how about I go and light the fire since it's getting rather chilly and your hands are white with cold?" She rubbed her fingers over his, before bringing his hand up to her lips.

Chance grabbed her and pulled her over onto his lap. Callie squealed and pretended to fight him but in all reality she was exactly where her heart yearned to be. A sexy cowboy of her own, a house the bank wouldn't come and take over, and a ranch that was going to get a dusting of snow. How much more could a girl dream of?

He kissed her passionately and held her on his knee as

they watched the sky slowly darken overhead. When the lights flickered on in the town down in the valley, Chance released her and they headed indoors to light the fire and prepare dinner.

Chapter Twelve

B Y THE TIME Callie and Chance crawled out of bed the next day the sky was overcast and the air frigid. She hurried through breakfast, determined to get a round done of the cow's paddock before the weather made it impossible to stay outside any longer. Last thing she wanted was to lose any calves to the freezing weather. They were far too valuable. Nothing Chance said could calm her down; she was hellbent on riding the paddock to make sure the stock was okay.

"Don't worry about me, I'll be fine. I'm rugged up and I have the horse and Sherbet with me. I won't be long, and then we can go and snuggle in front of the fire again and watch the snow blanket the ground."

Chance wrapped his arms around her, holding her close. He didn't want her to go out in the cold but she was taking her job seriously and for that he was proud of her. She knew what she was doing.

"If you don't come back in before lunch, I'll call Tyson. I'm betting snow will be here by then."

"You won't have to, I promise. One trip around the paddock and I'll be back before you know it." She kissed him soundly and pulled away, wiggling her gloved fingers at him before hurrying out the door with her dog at her heels.

Chance watched her hurry down to the barn and he was still standing at the window when ten minutes later she rode Sultan out of the barn and headed down to the cow paddock. He made himself a cup of coffee and hobbled into the living room and threw another couple of logs onto the fire before turning on the radio to distract himself from worrying about her.

An hour passed as he sat and looked into the flames, all but ignoring the chatter on the local station. Instead, Chance was trying to find the right words to tell his brothers what his plans were. But no matter how he worded it in his mind, it still sounded bad. He couldn't figure out how to tell them he hated his old life and longed for the simple pleasures of working his own ranch with his wife by his side. They would ask why he'd stayed on the tour as long as he had if it wasn't what he wanted. There was nothing he could say that would make it sound like he was doing it for himself when he had been propping them all up with his winnings. They wouldn't appreciate the way he'd stayed away.

What man would be happy to hear that? Certainly not his brothers. They all thought they were independent and could stand on their own two feet. Knowing he had done it to make up for his guilt at leaving them with their drunken father would cause a rift between the brothers he wasn't ready to deal with just yet, if ever. And now everyone was settled so to speak, he had the chance to change his life.

He glanced at his watch and cursed. Three hours had passed while he'd been sitting in front of the fire worrying about something he had no control over and as he'd predicted, snow had begun to fall in a gentle flutter. It might be best to just tell his brothers he'd had a change of heart and was over the high life he'd been leading the last twelve years. If he was careful, he could be convincing and make them believe him. What other choice did he have?

Chance got up and put more wood on the fire before heading into the kitchen to do the breakfast dishes. If Callie wasn't back by the time he'd finished, he was calling Tyson. The snow wasn't that heavy but it was getting thicker. Five long, drawn-out minutes later, she still hadn't shown up. Chance reached for the phone and called his brother.

"What do you mean, she hasn't come back? Hell, Chance. I told you she was wrong for the bloody job. Bet she's never seen a drop of snow in her damned life. I'll be right there." He slammed the phone down with a curse.

Chance looked down toward the barn, all but impossible to see now the snow was coming down harder. He paced the kitchen until he saw the lights of Tyson's truck coming toward the house.

When Tyson opened the truck door, Chance was waiting for him. "Where did she go? I'll take the truck down and if I can't find her, we'll have to call in reinforcements."

"Thanks. This is the first time she's seen snow. I should never have let her go out by herself in this."

"Worry about that later when I get back. So help me, Chance, this is going to get sorted one way or another. Stay indoors, I don't need to find you frozen to death against a bloody fence post."

Chance shut the door, cursing the bull that put him in this position. He couldn't get over the feeling of uselessness that swamped him when he couldn't get in and help.

BY THE TIME she saddled the horse earlier that morning and headed toward the paddock, the wind was coming at her sideways, bitter and knife-like. She pulled her hat further down over her face and huddled against Sultan's neck, trying to keep her face out of the biting wind.

A few white flakes landed on her jacket as she unhooked the gate into the paddock and Callie took a moment to gaze at them in wonder. She slipped off her glove and touched the flake with her fingers, watching it melt away to a spot of water. Another few dropped and then more followed. It was like being caught in a pillow fight with white duck feathers floating down from the clouds. Soon there was a steady rain of snowflakes with more than a few of them falling down the collar of her jacket to melt down her back.

She nudged the horse and they began their routine crisscross of the large paddock, making sure there were no cows in trouble and the calves that were already on the ground were making progress. She was prepared to move any unstable calves to the barn until they were able to follow their mothers and suckle freely. The last thing she wanted was to find a dead calf with a distraught mother when she could have saved it.

Sherbet ran ahead and got lost in the long grass. Callie cursed under her breath and hoped it wasn't trouble. She nudged Sultan and headed in the same direction, her head down, holding the brim of her hat to keep the snow out of her eyes. The chill of cold snowflakes down the back of her neck was starting to take the joy and shine out of the experience for her, and she wished she was back at the ranch house in front of the fire with Chance snuggling on the large rug watching the logs burn down to glowing. warm embers as they had last night.

She listened for the sound of barking and hoped the dog would make it easier for her to find whatever it was that had snaffled her attention. The soft flakes were falling faster and faster, making it difficult for Callie to see where she was going. Everywhere she looked was a sheet of white, making it impossible for her to gauge where she was in the paddock.

A sharp bark had her turning to the right. "Sherbet. Sherbet, where are you?" She called and called, hoping the dog would keep up its bark to guide her to where she was. After a couple of pauses, Callie honed in on her dog and managed to find her way to a clump of grass hiding a dirty white cow almost invisible against the snow covered ground.

Callie slid from the saddle and let the reins hang loose over Sultan's neck. She dropped to the ground and patted Sherbet. "Good girl. Well done." The cow wasn't moving and Callie touched her swollen stomach, hoping upon hope she and the calf were still alive. She could see its hooves protruding out of its mother and wondered why she had gone down.

By the time the small bull calf was pulled from the cow, Callie was exhausted. Her arms ached and she was freezing cold. With no other choice, she picked up the calf in her arms, hooked her hand in the reins, and started walking toward where she thought the gate was. Shivering with cold and weary beyond reason, she was relieved when she saw lights coming toward her.

Her brother-in-law pulled up and jumped out of the truck.

"What the fucking hell have you done? Chance is out of his mind with worry." Tyson's face was red with fury as he rounded on her. "I had to threaten him with violence to stop him taking the horse and coming to find you. What kind of irresponsible damned ranch manager are you anyway?"

"The kind who gets things done and doesn't let the stock die because of a touch of bad weather. Now is there anything I can do for you or are you just going to get in my way? I have to find this young man a bottle or a surrogate mother before we lose him too." Callie brushed past him and headed back to the barn following the tracks the truck left in the snow.

He pulled up beside her. "Get in. No need to make this any worse than it is."

"Piss off, leave me alone." She ignored him and trudged out of the paddock toward the barn. When she got there, she struggled to an empty stall, her legs wobbly with fatigue. She kicked the door open and walked in, dropping to her knees to place the shivering calf on the ground.

Grabbing a handful of hay, she rubbed the near-freezing animal down until it started to struggle and move under her administrations. "That's the way, fight, buddy. I don't want you to go the same way as your mama. Don't let me get frostbite for nothing now."

"Callie. What the hell happened out there? I was worried sick." Chance came hobbling into the barn, his face contorted with anger.

"Cow went down. She was halfway giving birth so I had to get this little guy out. She didn't make it." Callie looked up disappointed to see the anger on his face. "Any powdered milk around at all?"

He looked a little bit stunned but gathered himself. "Yeah, sure. In the feed bins there's always a bag of milk for cases like this. Should be a couple of bottles as well. Let me go and look."

"Nope, my job. You rest. Seems like you've already done

more than you should today anyway." Bitterness crept up her throat but she pushed it down. Any fool could see she was doing her job but still he snapped at her. She hurried toward the feed bins, ignoring the deathly looks she was getting from her brother-in-law. She could deal with him later, once the calf was settled and warm.

Tyson followed Chance and leaned over the edge of the stall, his face thunderous. "Chance, this is ridiculous. If that had been a local man you'd hired on, this would never have happened. And you damn well know they could have handled this situation a lot better than she did, too. Getting lost in the paddock, scaring the heck out of you. Come on, how much convincing do you need to get decent help? If I hadn't been available to come to the rescue, what would you have done, gone out yourself?" Tyson glared at her as she brushed past him and went to make a bottle up for the calf.

"I hear you, brother. We can talk about it later." He looked down at the calf struggling to find its feet. "Callie probably did the right thing. He'd have died alongside his mama if she hadn't found him and brought him in. At least she's managed to salvage something out of bad situation. Considering it's her first taste of snow, I'm proud of the way she's held up."

"What's one calf when it could have been you out there? Hell's teeth, you're injured and need to recuperate, not run around after the 'ranch manager.' Seems to me, you're going soft in your old age. Sure it wasn't your head Terror stood on and not your hip?"

Chance pushed his brother against the wall of the stall and put his face up against Tyson's. "Give it a rest. Now. I made the decision to hire her on and I fully expect you to respect that. Callie knows what she's doing and so do I. I don't need you telling me what to do."

She walked back with the bottle in her hand, shaking it to warm the formula and make sure it was mixed properly. "Thanks, boss, but if your brother has any issues he's more than welcome to deal with me face-to-face. I can sort out my own problems. Just let me feed this little guy and then he can have my undivided attention."

Callie met Tyson's gaze and didn't glance away from the hateful look he gave her. "After all, the animals come first in this job, not a man's pissy attitude." She put the bottle on the ground and wrapped her arms around the calf, encouraging it to its feet. She held her hands under its belly until it was more stable on its wobbly legs before slipping a couple of fingers into its mouth. The warm tongue whipped around her fingers and started to suck, banging into the palm of her hand with insistent nudges.

Callie smiled, breathing a sigh of relief that he was ready and willing to nurse. She picked up the bottle and slid the teat between her fingers, easing them out of the calf's mouth as it latched onto the teat. The sucking noises filled the quiet barn, easing the fear from her shoulders. It made all the anger pointed in her direction, worthwhile.

When he was finished, he turned and tried to nudge her hands looking for more milk. Callie laughed, rubbing his little body to keep him warm. "Okay if I use a saddle blanket to wrap around him for the night? He needs all the warmth he can get in this weather."

"We have calf coats in the tack room. They should be hanging up. Let me go and get you one." Chance hobbled off before she could protest.

Tyson walked into the stall and glared at her. "If you do anything so damned stupid again and cause him anymore grief, so help me, I'll run you off the ranch myself. Do I make myself clear?"

Callie looked up at him, intensely sorry they couldn't tell Tyson the real reason she was here. "I'm doing my job the best as I can. I'm not ashamed of the fact this is the first snow I've seen, but it doesn't make any difference. I had to save that calf and I did it. If you don't like it, tough luck, pal, because you aren't my employer, he is." Sherbet eased her way between her new owner and the man threatening her, a low growl coming from her throat. Callie rested a hand on the dog's head, hoping to calm her before she reacted. Biting Tyson wouldn't help matters at all but the thought of it warmed her.

"I bet you think he's an easy grab, a famous rodeo star loaded with cash and a busted leg. Start out working the ranch and ease your way into his bed." He leaned closer and poked his finger into her shoulder, his hot breath rolling over her face. "Let me tell you something for free, girl. You're not his type, not in the slightest. You don't even come close to what Chance likes in a woman, so do yourself a favor and go back to where you belong cause it ain't here in Marietta."

Tyson stepped away as Chance came back with a cover for the calf. He shuffled into the stall and handed it to Callie, waiting while she rugged the newborn up. "I'll have to come and feed him every four hours, otherwise he's not going to make it."

"We can set an alarm. Now let's get you back into the house to get warm and dry. No point you getting sick." Chance stood aside to let her walk out, shutting the door behind them.

"Thanks for coming over, brother. I appreciate it." Chance patted Tyson on the back.

"I have to unsaddle Sultan. I'll be up soon." Callie hurried over to the horse, and rubbed her hand over his nose, ignoring the chatter from the two brothers. The wind howled when the door opened and they walked out, Tyson's mood no better than when he'd arrived. She took the horse's bridle off and the saddle, making sure to rug him up well before shutting him in his stall.

When she was finished, Sherbet was sitting waiting for her. Callie crouched down and hugged the dog, letting her disappointment have free rein for a moment. "If it wasn't for you, we wouldn't be here now. Such a good girl, aren't you?"

She sat crouched with her dog sucking up the boundless love, knowing the animal would never treat her the way the two brothers had done.

Chapter Thirteen

O NCE SHE WALKED inside, Chance insisted she take off her boots and jacket and have a long hot shower before sitting in front of the fireplace. When Callie came down with dry clothes on, a bowl of soup and hot toast was set out on a tray and it was sitting on the table in front of the roaring fire and she gravitated toward it.

"Canned I'm afraid, but better than nothing." He reached out, pulling Callie into his chest, his arms wrapped around her. "You had me so damned worried, you know. I couldn't bear to think about what would have happened if you got hurt or lost in that storm."

Alone with only her, he seemed to be a different person, the earlier snappy mood gone as soon as Tyson drove away.

"Hmm, it's kind of different to what I'm used to. I have to say I think I prefer the heat to the cold, although looking at it from inside the house it's kind of pretty." She snuggled against his chest, her gaze on the white curtain of snow outside the window blocking them in from the outside world. "There was no way I wasn't coming back to this either." Callie lifted her mouth to his. With a passion fraught with images of loss, she slid her hands up under her husband's shirt. His nipples pebbled when she ran her fingertips over the small beads of flesh and Chance groaned.

"I'm sorry I snapped at you before. You scared me." He kissed her lips. "You need to eat something warm."

She nibbled at his ear, laughing as the goose bumps rolled over his skin and he was unable to stop her. "I need this more. The soup can wait." Callie pulled him down onto the rug in front of the fireplace, straddling him, careful not to place too much pressure on his hip. Button after button was undone and she spread his shirt open, exposing the wide expanse of chest and stomach to her hungry gaze.

She kissed his throat, making her way down to the small trail of hair that disappeared under his jeans. With hurried moves, Callie undid his belt buckle before popping the button on the blue denim jeans. "Lift up, cowboy."

Chance lifted his hips and she slid his jeans and boxers down to his knees, exposing his need to her greedy eyes.

"Take it all off for me." He pulled her shirt from her old, cozy track pants and pushed it up so he could reach her full, soft breasts. Chance tweaked the nipples as she lifted her arms and pulled the shirt up before throwing it on the floor beside them.

"Come down here." Chance opened his mouth and took in one of her nipples as she leaned down over him. She shuffled lower so she was sitting over his erection, moving around carefully but with enough pressure to make him groan in pleasure. "Oh, my fucking God, stay right there." He switched nipples, lathering as much attention on her other breast as he did on the first.

"I need you right now." Callie gasped and moved her heated core over his erection. She lifted herself and reached for him. Slowly, inch by inch, she lowered herself until he was buried deep inside her. The warmth of her body wrapped around him, almost sending him over the edge. He wanted to savor the moment, but knew they both needed sex hard and fast after this morning's tension.

Chance started to move his hips, thankful the pain was almost nonexistent now. He glanced up into Callie's face. Her eyes were closed and she had a look of unbridled joy on her face. Her mouth was open, emitting small sounds of pleasure that reminded him of a cat's purr. She started to move faster, pushing herself down harder and spreading her legs to take him as far as she could.

He gripped her hips and upped the pace, plunging deeper and harder with each stroke.

SHE ROLLED OFF of Chance and onto her back, staring up at the ceiling above them. It might be snowing outside but in the lounge it was hot. She knew that was more to do with the *great panic overalmost losing you* sex they'd just shared and not the fire crackling in the hearth in front of them. Callie glanced at her half naked cowboy and reached for his hand. "Thanks. I really needed that." They lay together until the pangs of hunger made it impossible for her not to move.

As she rose to her feet, she gathered her clothes. Callie dressed in front of the flames before helping Chance pull up his jeans. She stood over him, smiling as he made lewd remarks of where they should spend the rest of their afternoon, making the most of the bad weather.

"You're forgetting I have a job to do and a small bull calf that needs to be fed in a couple of hours. As much as I'd like to do what you suggest, not gonna happen." She looked at the cold soup and picked up the bowl. "Might have to reheat this, back soon."

In the kitchen, she put the bowl in the microwave and walked over to Sherbet who was sleeping on an old horse blanket Chance had given her. Callie leaned down and patted the dog's head; forever thankful she had been chosen by the beautiful girl and had decided to not take one of the pups. "You are the best dog out, you know that right?"

Sherbet licked Callie's hand and snuggled back down to sleep, content in the knowledge they were warm and safe inside.

After washing her hands, Callie made a plate of hot buttered toast and put it on a tray with the soup and two spoons before heading back into the lounge where her husband was still sitting on the rug in front of the fire. She put the tray down in front of him and sat cross legged, taking a piece of toast.

"I'm sorry you were so worried about me." She took a bite, the melted butter running down her chin. Chance leaned over and licked it up before placing a soft kiss on her lips.

"I was frantic and not being stupid enough to try and get on a horse myself, I had no choice but to call on Tyson. I'm sorry he was such an ass to you and I was no better. He's just being protective, I know that, but it might be wise if I came up with another reason why I stayed on the tour and not because I wanted the money for them to get a good start in life."

"Could be a good idea. I'd hate for this to drag on for too long. I can only take so much crap from people who have no idea what they're talking about." Callie picked up a spoon and tried the soup. "Yummo, have some." She dipped her toast in, soaking up the fragrant juices before popping it in her mouth. "How come he's not married himself? If he had his own wife, he might not have the time or inclination to worry about you so much."

A look of wonder crossed over Chance's eyes. "Hell, I never thought of that. He's never mentioned a girlfriend and I've been too focused on myself to even give it a thought. I might bring it up next time I see him. Come to think of it, none of my brothers are hitched with the exception of Rory who's now widowed." He picked up a piece of toast. "Did I tell you he's coming home?"

"Nope, you didn't."

"I spoke to him yesterday. Suggested he move back here so he's close to family and he let out that he's given his notice and is applying in Marietta. We could use another good deputy like him in town."

Callie smiled at the enthusiasm Chance showed at the mention of his brother. She hoped she could see her sisters again before too long. It would be nice to have them over to stay and show them where she worked and now lived. Sadly that would take too much of her precious wage and wasn't going to happen. A fleeting sadness crept up her throat.

"What's that frown for?" Chance cupped her chin in his hand.

"I was thinking about my sisters. They don't know I answered a mail order bride advert. I told them it was a job. Not sure they're old enough to understand what I did just yet."

"You can always get them over for a holiday and break it to them when they're here. Once we win them over with my charm and the ranch that is." He grinned and Callie let the sadness slide away.

There was no point telling Chance because he'd probably want to pay for their fares, something that wasn't going to happen. Her sisters would fall in love with him because they wouldn't be able to help themselves and when it came time for the contract to wind up and Chance to swear off love, they'd only get hurt more. She would deal with it when the time was right. Now she had to finish her soup and get rugged up to go and feed the calf again. Every four hours—it was going to be a long night.

Chapter Fourteen

CHANCE OPENED HIS eyes and rolled over, reaching for his wife. The spot where her head rested last night on the pillow was cold and empty.

He sat up and called her name. "Callie, are you there?" When she didn't reply he lay back.

She must be out feeding the calf again. He looked over at the window, and breathed a sigh of relief when he saw the snow had stopped. The clouds were still there, but Chance could see patches of blue peeking through. He might as well get up and go and see how his dear wife was coping with the calf.

As he pulled up his jeans, Chance noticed how much better his hip was feeling. The stiffness had gone out of it and he could walk to the bathroom without the cane. Must be one of the benefits of married life. Sex kept his body supple and loose. He snorted a laugh. Wait until he told Callie that. Not that he thought she would mind, considering she was to blame a lot of the time for initiating more than half of the times they had sex.

The sound of her singing to herself made him smile when he walked into the barn, her off-tune voice heavy with the Australian twang he was growing to love. The door was open on the horse stalls and both of them were outside in the paddock, snuffling around to find a blade of green grass under the rapidly melting snow. Chance stood at the door and watched her pitchforking the dirty shavings into a wheel barrow. When she noticed him, she grinned and his heart soared. Who would have thought choosing a bride over the internet would work out so well for him? Mail order brides had been something he associated with strange people who liked to hide away and not be social. Older men who tended to choose brides from impoverished countries who were willing to overlook their new husband's weird behavior.

Once his brothers found out the truth, he would take flak from them. He'd gladly take any amount of ribbing so long as they didn't get offended with his reasons for staying away.

"Hey, cowboy. You're looking mighty fine and rested this morning." She leaned on the pitchfork and watched him move closer.

Just her gaze alone had his cock twitching in his jeans. He'd never met anyone that had that kind of control over him. The sexy cowgirl from the strange land down under was going to find herself on her back in a clean stall if she wasn't careful. The thought warmed his blood.

"Uh, Chance, hold on. You have that look in your eye

and you're not using your cane. What's going on?" She backed away, laughing as he held his hands out to grab her.

With a squeal, Callie ran over to the stall with the calf in it, opening the door and slipped in before closing it behind her. "Wait, just wait. I have work to do here."

"Really? Well, so do I." He looked over the door at the calf nudging at her legs searching for a feed. "Hey, good job. He's looking wonderful." Suddenly Chance was sidetracked. The little bull was the image of his father, Terror. Seemed the old guy was good for something other than inflicting pain after all. "Well, I'll be. I never noticed it last night but he's a little beauty."

"Yeah, he is. It's a shame about his mama though, but it would seem he's going to pull through. I'll give him another bottle since it's only about half an hour before he's due anyway. Don't think he's going to let me get away from him without it." She ran her hand over his silken ears. "I did a quick ride around the paddock earlier. Another couple of calves born overnight but they're up and suckling fine. We'll have to go out and bury the cow before the wild animals come in and cause any grief. Don't want them taking calves as an easy feed."

"No, we don't need that. I can bring out the tractor and dig a hole."

"So long as you're up to it. Don't want you overdoing things and getting a strip torn off you from the doctor." She opened the door and slid out, avoiding the calf.

Chance watched her make up the bottle. When she returned to the stall, the calf had her struggling to stay on her feet for the short amount of time it took it to empty the formula. Chance's libido was working overtime and it was all Callie's fault for looking so damned sexy and getting his imagination running wild. When she stepped out, he took her arm and guided her into the next empty stall.

"What do you think you're doing? I have jobs to do and a boss that will whip my butt if they don't get done." She tried to act offended when he pinned her to the wall but he knew she was loving it as much as he was. Chance undid the buckle on her belt, popped the button on her jeans and pulled them down around her knees. "Turn around, baby, this is going to be hard and fast."

The look in her eyes gave away just how hot and horny she was. With a whimper of lust, not fear, Callie turned and faced the wall, her butt poking out and exposed in his direction. He undid his belt and dropped his pants, pushing himself against her, his cock hard and ready. Callie perched herself up on her heels and leaned forward more, bending at the waist so her bottom was raised. When she spread her legs and bared herself to Chance, he positioned his cock at her moist entrance and pushed himself all the way home.

Her sigh of pleasure broke the silence of the barn and the groans coming from her lips were the only noise he could hear as he slammed into her, crying out with his own release when he came. She peaked just after him, stifling a squeal that somehow turned to a grunt that went on for a long shuddering sigh. Chance rested with his arms around her belly while they both got their breath back.

"You sure know how to please a girl, cowboy."

"I aim to please, ma'am. Part of the cowboy creed." Chance pulled out of her and reached for his pants, pulling them up.

CALLIE TURNED AROUND, still breathing heavily. "You know, I have this fantasy you might be able to help me out with. There's this cowboy who drives me wild." She picked a piece of hay from the rack and poked it between her teeth, glancing at him as she stood there with her lower body still exposed. "I want him to drag me up the hay loft and have his wicked way with me, but I'm afraid we'll be caught."

"And that's putting you off?" He did up his belt buckle, his gaze on her body.

"No, not at all. It adds to the pleasure and excitement of it all."

"Well, tell you what, little lady. Let's go and do some of your jobs while I think about letting that cowboy loose to pleasure you and then, if you're really good, I'll organize it for another day when said cowboy is feeling up to climbing that ladder. Does that meet with your approval?"

"I guess if that's the way it has to be." She pouted and

pulled up her jeans, then leaned in for a kiss. "Let's get going so we can sit back and enjoy the view from the lounge after we're done." Callie slid out of the stall and called to Sherbet who was sleeping over near the door. "Lead me to the machinery shed and let's get this poor old cow buried."

The ground was hard where the cow had died but with the tractor, Chance managed to dig a fairly decent hole and push the cow in. Once she was covered with dirt, Callie breathed a sigh of relief. She had no urge to see a cougar any time soon.

Once the animals were all fed and her jobs done for the day, they headed for the house where the fire was still glowing in the hearth. Now was a good time to learn more about each other. Callie stood in the kitchen making a big pot of vegetable soup while she grilled Chance about his past exploits in the IBR.

"You know, I never knew it was such a lucrative sport. We have them at home, but I'm not sure it pays the same kind of money."

"It does pay extremely well at the top level but the majority of my income now comes from sponsorship and my product line. It's chugging away nicely now on its own. Took a while to build up but now I don't have to worry too much about it apart from the odd promotional day or advertisements that need tweaking. As for the IBR side of things, it's almost a national sport in Montana. I was thinking of running small classes for kids that want to learn the ropes. Just one of the things I've been tossing over in my mind to make this place pay for itself."

"Sounds like a good idea. I'm sure there would be plenty of people interested. Although I reckon with the breeding you plan on doing, there'll be enough to keep both of us busy." Callie tossed in a large tub of chicken stock and stirred the pot, smelling the aromas filling the kitchen.

"When this hip heals good and I get the pins out, how about a trip to buy more cattle? If I'm going to do this properly we need a heap more cows. What we're running now we can more than triple. We have the land for it so we may as well."

"Sure and I agree, but won't you then have to take on more hands? I doubt between us we will be able to keep up with everything and I'm only here for a year."

His gaze darkened at her words. "I was rather hoping to talk a couple of the local boys into coming to work for me once we had things settled. Ralph, my friend is still on the tour. I'd thought about asking him if he wanted to come and work on the ranch when his time is up and he's sick of the life."

"Did all of your brothers leave home as soon as they were able to?" Callie sniffed the aroma, watching the soup come to a soft simmer.

"Yeah. Guess they got sick of the old man too eventually. Can't blame them. Not like I hung around so they didn't have a good example to follow."

Callie kept her opinion to herself. It would be good for Chance to have his brothers at home, but she wondered if there was any way she could encourage him to mend the rift between he and his father.

"Ralph and I went to school and grew up together and not long after I took off, so did he. Until his father decides to let him have a say in the family ranch, he has no interest in going back there. Pretty good chance he'd work for me if I asked him to."

"I'm sure you'll find someone capable and able."

Chapter Fifteen

CHANCE WOKE UP to Sherbet barking at the door of the kitchen. Callie was in the shower, singing away loudly and off key. She wouldn't hear anyway being under the water. He pulled on a pair of jeans and did them up as he hurried down the stairs to the kitchen.

"Shush, Sherbet." There was a woman standing on the porch looking out over the ranch and his stomach tied up in knots. *No fucking way, this wasn't happening.*

He unlocked the door and opened it wide.

A pair of stunning green eyes locked onto his and with a squeal, the woman threw herself into his arms. "Chance, I was so worried when you didn't call me. Seriously, terrified doesn't even begin to say what went through my head when I heard you'd been hurt." She clung to him, her head resting on his shoulder as the small sobs reached his ears.

In the months after his accident and operation he'd managed to avoid her. Looked like his luck had run out.

He pushed her away and looked into her eyes. "Libby, who told you where I lived?"

"What? Oh, um, I really don't remember. But that's not important." She brushed past him into the kitchen and pulled up short when Sherbet bared her teeth, a low growl coming from her throat. "Shouldn't that beast be outside, Chance. My allergies, you know how bad they are." Libby stood with her hands up around her face, waiting for him to save her.

He spoke to the dog. "Outside girl. Go on." Sherbet trotted out he shut the door but not before he saw the suitcase on the porch. This was going to be harder than he thought. "Why are you here, Libby?"

"You need me, darling. I heard about your accident and caught the first plane I could find that came to this little backwards town of yours." She looked around the house and poked her head into the living room "You should have had someone find me, you know. I could have been by your side months ago helping you go through rehab and everything." She sniffed and wiped away a tear. "Your brother told me you lived up here, he gave me a lift up the driveway. His was the only number in the phone book and you weren't answering your cell phone."

On purpose. "You can't stay. I don't need or want you here." He was determined to get rid of her. Tyson dropped her off, he could come back and get her.

She pouted at him, her eyes going wide with wonder. "But that's not possible, darling. I need to look after you. We mean so much to each other after all. How would it look if word got out your girlfriend left you in your time of need? It's bad enough that I was away shooting my latest movie when you were hurt but now I'm back and ready to look after you."

"You're not my girlfriend. We had a good few dates and got on fine, but that was all there was to it." He hoped Callie wouldn't come down the stairs just yet.

"Don't be so nasty, darling. You know you don't mean it. I get how you like your independence but really, it's time we got married, don't you think?" She ran a scarlet fingernail over the island counter, pulling a face. "This place could do with a serious revamp though. Not that I want to be caught living in the sticks but, Chance, for a holiday home it will do, I suppose."

"Stop. Get it through your head, Libby. You are not my girlfriend, you are leaving and we are never, ever getting married. I don't need you to look after me." He ran a hand through his hair. "I have someone here, someone who—"

"Oh, I know. Your brother told me. She almost got you killed out in a snow drift." She *tsked* and shook her head. "Fancy hiring a manager from Australia. I don't know what you were thinking about, darling. It's obvious to me that you've missed me. You wouldn't act like this if you didn't." She looked up the staircase. "If you could get your manager to bring my bag up, I'd appreciate it. The flight was exhausting and so early in the morning, too. I hope you appreciate the sacrifice I made to get here."

"Stop right there. Don't move." Chance reached for the phone and dialed his brother's number. When the house phone went to voice mail, he dialed the cell.

"Chance, nice surprise?" Tyson's cheery voice grated on his nerves.

"No, it wasn't and if you'd bothered to let me know, I'd have told you to put her back on the damned plane. She's the last person I want here right now."

"That's no way to talk about your fiancé."

"She isn't and never will be my fiancé. Come back here and pick her up."

"No can do, brother. I'm on my way to pick up some horses. Won't be home til tomorrow."

Chance hung up the phone, furious at Tyson. He looked up when he heard footsteps coming down the stairs. Callie. *Fuck it.*

CALLIE SKIPPED DOWN the stairs but slowed as she reached the bottom. Chance's angry voice came from the kitchen followed by a plaintive whine—a feminine whine at that. Her senses on alert, she slowed her steps, listening.

"Now I'm here we can finally let the press know what's going on between us. I tell you, Chance, they've been hounding me day and night asking when we're going to announce our engagement to the public." She hurried on, ignoring the protests coming from Chance. "Of course, I had to tell my manager first. He'll write up an official release and then we can organize a photo shoot. I've decided we need to go back to the city for that though. I seriously want to get as much traction from this as possible. Whip up interest in the wedding of the decade. I might get another movie deal if I play my cards right."

Callie walked into the kitchen when her husband's new "fiancé" paused for breath. Chance's eyes rolled and he put his finger to his lips. "Callie, good morning. I was just about to take Libby back the airport. She's come all this way to help out, but I've tried to tell her you and I have everything under control."

Libby turned on Callie, fire in her eyes. "How dare you put my future husband in harm's way." She walked over and poked a well-manicured finger at Callie. "You should be ashamed of yourself. Call yourself a ranch manager, huh. I bet you're trying to latch onto him because of who he is. I know your type, missy. It won't work."

The woman's venom shocked her, taking the normally fast-witted Callie by surprise. "I'm not sure that this is any of your business."

Libby glared at her and stalked over to Chance, slipping her arm through his. "What affects my future husband affects me. If you can't do your job without putting him in danger, you'll have to be replaced." She pouted up at Chance. "Won't she, darling?"

"Look, Libby. I've already told you, we're not together and never will be. You need to leave."

"But you can't mean that, darling. Not after what we went through the last time we were together. The plans we made and the seeds we sowed wrapped in each other's arms." She let tears fill her eyes and dropped her hand to cup her flat stomach. "Our new life is just beginning. You can't throw us out now."

"What?" Chance stared at Libby, his gaze dropping to her stomach before glancing in Callie's direction, a look of horror on his face.

Callie couldn't stand to hear anymore. She brushed past him and opened the door, slamming it behind her. Sherbet was sitting on the porch waiting for her and together they ran down toward the barn.

The bastard. How dare he marry her when he'd been making a life with that, that fluffy, airheaded damned actress? If he'd only wanted a ranch manager and not a wife, she would still have moved over for the job. That was one of the reasons he didn't want to tell her. None of this made sense. Why would he marry her if he only wanted her to look after the place? Did he think she wouldn't share his bed without a ring? His bullshit excuse that she would look after things if she had a stake in it didn't fly for her, not anymore. There had been no reason to lie to get her here. It was all a sick joke on his part and Callie didn't find any part of it funny. She swallowed a sob, her hand over her mouth trying to stifle the noise.

They had seemed so good together. Almost too good to be true how they'd hit it off in and out of bed. She felt dirty and used, someone to throw away when a better model came to town. And his brother had brought her up here. Bloody typical. He'd been against Callie from the start and made it well-known, too. She might have guessed he'd do something like this to get rid of her. And Chance appeared to be in on it no matter what he was telling her.

It would seem it was time for her to move on and find another job regardless of the contract she'd signed. There had to be a way to get out of it and, damn it, she'd find it.

There must be another ranch around that needed a good worker. Preferably one where there weren't any lying cowboys who claimed they wanted to marry her and insinuate they wanted to raise a family away from the limelight. Didn't Chance say Jethro's grandfather needed help? She'd find out who and where he was and try to work something out. Callie pushed open the barn door and hurried inside. She let go the sobs rising in her throat, doubling over in anguish as the tears had their way.

Fancy falling for Chance's line. It seemed too stupid now she thought about it. Someone famous like him wanting the quiet life away from the spotlight and with a small-time farmer like her to make a future. Why would she even think that could be real? Things like that only ever happened in fairy tales and certainly not to people like her. It was a shame she would have to have the marriage annulled. With any luck, a Las Vegas wedding wouldn't be legal. She'd check it out.

The bleating of the calf snapped her out of the self-pity wave she was riding. Callie wiped her hand across her eyes. She had jobs to do, animals to feed and check on, before she could worry about herself and how to get out of this sham of a marriage. She fed the calf first, then the horses before downing a large drink of water from the tap outside the barn. There was no way she was going back to the house for breakfast until decisions had been made.

By the time Callie was ready to ride the paddock and check the cows, she had calmed down. Analyzing things made her feel more in control of the situation. More subdued than normal, she saddled Sultan and headed out, ignoring Chance who was making his way down the drive toward the barn with his *girlfriend* watching him from the porch.

Callie kicked her heels up and took off, determined to have more time to try and sort out her jumbled emotions before talking to him again.

Chapter Sixteen

CHANCE SAT WAITING for Callie to come back, determined to have his say and let her know what was going on before he took Libby back to the airport for her plane. Pregnant or not, she wasn't staying. More than prepared to support her if it was his child, he would make sure she had everything she needed but not at the ranch. Not with his wife already living there. What a monumental fuck-up.

Libby had been fun to be around when he was on the tour looking for a good time. She was flirty and not shy about wanting to drag him into her bed. They had a good time but that was all it was and he thought she knew that. Chance never said anything to her about settling down. He hadn't mentioned it to any women he'd dated and if the marriage word ever came up, he didn't repeat the date, preferring to move onto greener pastures.

He'd left Libby at the house after making sure her seat was booked for the afternoon flight and she'd sulkily agreed he would drive her. Once she realized he was determined to get rid of her, the theatrical tears had dried up.

Callie was out on Sultan doing her check on the cows and calves and he knew she would be back soon. It was just a matter of waiting for her to get his story across. She had to come to her senses and believe him, she just had to. Callie was the only wife he wanted and he wouldn't let her go without a fight; that much he knew well before her contract was up.

Chance leaned on the paddock gate, his gaze roving over the young bulls. A bark caught his attention and he looked over his shoulder to where Sherbet was running toward him. He could see his wife riding closer and he smiled. This had to work in his favor. He couldn't lose her. He wouldn't lose her.

Sherbet sailed over the wire and ran toward Chance, pausing to sniff his leg before pushing through the fence toward the bull stomping one of his front feet in the dirt. Terror stood still, his head hanging low. Sherbet ran toward him and slunk down low to the ground the closer she got. When the dog was ten meters away, she lay down and froze in position.

Chance pushed his hat back and looked. The bull wasn't worried about the dog, which was strange in itself. He'd never seen Terror not attack anything that got too close to him. He climbed up on the fence to get a better look and saw the tangle of old wire wrapped around the bull's back legs.

Bloody hell. Without giving himself time to think,

Chance acted on instinct and climbed the fence, making his way calmly toward the bull. Terror snorted but made no attempt to attack. *Which means he knows he's in trouble and needs help.* His voice low and soothing, Chance walked toward the back of his bull but kept his distance until he reached the rear of the animal.

The wire was rusted and tangled, both back legs caught up and bleeding. He wondered how long Terror had been caught like this.

The beat of horse hooves thundered over the paddock and he looked up. Callie sat on Sultan at the gate, watching him work the legs free from the discarded fencing wire. Chance lifted a bleeding leg and hurried to pull away the tangle. He breathed a sigh of relief when Terror stamped his now free hooves. Clutching the wire, Chance eased away from him.

Sherbet made her way on her belly between the bull and the man, giving him time to make a break for the fence.

Callie cried out as the sound of thundering hooves pounded the ground behind Chance. He turned to look over his shoulder to see the huge grey bull charging down on him. He threw himself down on the ground hoping to avoid the sharp horns angled his way. The last thing he heard as he sailed through the air was the scream coming from his wife.

SHE WATCHED INDISBELIEF as Chance tried to get the wire from around the bull's legs. She would have herded him into the small holding pen before attempting anything quite so foolish. After all, he was aggressive as Chance knew from experience. What the heck was he thinking? A scream rose in her throat as the bull charged Chance when he tried to walk away. Even Sherbet attempted to come between them but it made no difference.

She looked on in horror as her husband threw himself on the ground only to be picked up and thrown through the air. He landed, hitting the dirt hard. Callie waited for him to get up and escape the bull but he didn't move. Terror pawed at the ground and ducked his head down, ready to attack again.

Callie turned the horse, rode to the gate, and slipped the latch, pushing her way through. She kicked Sultan's ribs and headed straight for the bull, waving her hat and screaming at the top of her lungs. She rode between bull and man, pushing the animal further away from the prone body lying still in the grass.

"Move, you big bastard. Move I say." She herded Terror away from Chance toward the holding yard, not stopping until he was forced inside and the gate was shut behind him. She hurried back to Chance and jumped from the horse before it stilled. Callie crouched beside him. "Chance, please, please be alright."

Sherbet barked as a flash of red outside the fence caught her attention. Libby stood there, her dress blowing in the breeze.

"Go back to the house and call an ambulance. Now!" Callie screamed orders at her until the woman turned and did as she was told.

Chance remained still and unconscious on the ground. There was a smear of blood across his temple but that was the only mark she could see on him. He was breathing, so there was nothing she could do but wait for help to come and pray that he lived.

Callie sat holding his hand until the siren sounded. The ambulance barreled up the driveway and she stood up, waving her arms as they drove past the house. She stood back as the paramedics drove through the paddock and jumped out. "He's unconscious but breathing. The bull threw him and he landed hard. Please hurry." Tears filled her eyes now the shock was setting in.

"Don't worry, ma'am. He's in good hands." They checked his pupils and his breathing before rolling him over to look for major injuries. It seemed like hours before they glanced at each other and lifted Chance onto a stretcher, strapping him down. As they pushed the gurney to the door of the ambulance, Libby hurried over.

"I'm coming, too. He's my fiancé." She glanced at Callie, a hard gleam in her eyes and climbed in beside Chance.

The driver turned to look at Callie. "We'll be taking him into town to Marietta Hospital. They can decide what to do with him from there." He slammed the door and with the sirens screaming, took off with her husband.

Callie stood shell-shocked. She should be the one at Chance's side, not the woman who'd arrived this morning throwing Callie's world into disarray. Making the decision to follow galvanized her into action. She grabbed the horse and hurried to the barn, unsaddling him before letting him out into the paddock. She fed the calf, knowing he would survive if she missed the next feed now he was on his feet and warm and dry.

Callie hurried to the house and changed into clean clothes before telling Sherbet to stay. On impulse, she grabbed the phone book, checked for his number, and then called Tyson, leaving a message on his answering machine. She snatched up the keys to Chance's truck and headed into town to find the hospital. It wasn't hard to follow signs in the small town. At the reception desk, she asked for him by name and was shown to a waiting room where Libby sat, shredding a tissue on her lap.

"What are you doing here?" She glared at Callie daring her to answer.

"Have you heard anything? How is he?"

"No. Not that it's any of your business. If you'd done your job properly, he wouldn't be in here. I hope he fires you and if doesn't, I will."

"It's not your place to do anything." Callie wasn't going to let go of her husband without a fight. Seeing him on the ground had shown her what she already suspected. She couldn't leave after the contract finished and she would do everything she could to make Chance fall in love with her while she had time. Starting right now.

"Now you look here. Chance and I have an understanding and we're going to be—"

She broke off as a doctor in green scrubs entered the waiting room. "Relatives of Chance Watson?"

They both stepped forward.

Libby spoke first. "I'm his fiancé. What can you tell me, doctor?"

"We've done a scan. No broken bones but he has a bleed on the brain. We need to operate and release pressure. Are there no relatives close by?"

"I called his brother and left a message." Callie ignored the look from Libby. "Is there anything we can do for him?"

"I need papers signed so we can go ahead and operate. Can you call him again? We don't have much time."

"But, Doctor, can't I sign, being his fiancé?" Libby pushed her way in front of the doctor trying to block Callie out of the way.

He shook his head. "I'm afraid not. I need a legally binding agreement here."

"I can sign it." Callie crossed her arms and looked the doctor in the eye. "I'm his wife."

"What? No, you can't be." Libby paled, staggered back and dropped into a chair.

"We were married in Las Vegas a few weeks ago. Chance

hasn't had time to share the news with his family just yet."

"Fine. I'll organize the paperwork and we can proceed." The doctor looked between the two women and shaking his head in confusion, walked away leaving them to sort out their problems.

"How could he do this to me?" Libby put a hand over her forehead and leaned back in the chair. "I had it all planned out. Where we would get married and the house we would buy. My next movie role and our promotional tour together. What am I going to do now? How am I going to tell my fans that my life has been ruined?"

"Your fans? Look, lady, I'm not giving up my husband without a fight but I will make sure he knows I'll help him support your child. As far as your public life, I don't give a toss about how you look to your fans. That's your problem." Callie turned away, horrified by the shallowness of the woman.

She was more concerned about how she looked than her apparent love for Chance. No wonder he wanted to get away from the shallowness of the people he was connected to on the tour. It would have driven Callie crazy in no time. She placed more importance on genuine relationships than the woman flicking though her phone and no doubt updating her status.

Callie signed the papers when they were brought out, then sat down in the chair to wait. Each time the door opened she would stand up, hoping for good news. After a couple of muffled phone calls, Libby gave her a deadly glare, tossed her head, and walked out, muttering to herself. Callie sighed with relief and took advantage of the solitude. She ran over the conversations she'd had with Chance and the plans they'd made for their next year together, hoping to get a rein on her emotions before Libby came back but an hour passed and she didn't return.

Footsteps pounded down the hallway and Callie looked up expectantly. Tyson strode into the room. "What the hell's going on? I got your message and then a mad phone call from Libby to tell me you just about got Chance killed."

Chapter Seventeen

CALLIE TOOK A deep breath. She wasn't going to take anymore insults from her brother in law, no matter how angry he got. Secrets be damned, she would stand up for herself. "Chance did it by himself."

"Don't give me that. He knows how dangerous that damned bull is. Libby told me you were in the paddock first, Chance came in to save your sorry ass. I knew he'd made a mistake hiring you on. Nothing but bloody trouble." He took a step closer to her and poked out his finger as if winding up for another attack.

The door opened and the doctor walked out, pulling off his surgical cap. "Mrs. Watson. He came through okay, still a bit groggy but he's asking to see you. I'll let you have five minutes and then he needs to rest."

"What the heck?"

Callie stood up and walked past Tyson but he grabbed her arm. "This isn't over and so help me, if you've duped my brother, you will be on the next plane out of here." She wrenched herself free and followed the doctor. He led her into a darkened room where a nurse checked vital signs and Chance lay still, a bandage around his head and a drip snaked into his arm. His face was deathly pale and his eyes closed.

"Talk to him. He was awake in recovery so he should respond."

Tears filled Callie's eyes and she stepped forward, pulling up the chair beside his bed. She reached for his hand, gripping it tightly between hers. His skin was cold and clammy. She brought his hand up to her face, kissing the cool skin before cradling it against her cheek. His eyelids fluttered and he tried to focus on her.

"Callie…"

"Shh, it's okay. You're in hospital, Chance. Terror gave you a hiding and they had to operate to release the pressure on your brain." She reached over to take his other hand. "The doctor said you're going to be fine. Rest up and get better, okay?"

He licked his lips and tried to focus on her face. "About Libby, she's lying, I know she is." He blinked and focused on her again. "I called her out on it before I came down to see you, and got sidetracked by Terror before I had a chance to talk to you. I don't think she's pregnant, but she wouldn't confirm or deny it. Just wants what she can't have."

"Chance, don't worry about that now. We can deal with her when you're better."

"I needed to tell you. I don't want you to leave me."

"I had no intention of leaving you even if she is pregnant. I'd stand by you. I decided that when I was out riding the paddock. I even convinced myself I'd help you raise the kid if it came to that. I couldn't let that come between us, Chance. I love you."

"Love you more." He squeezed her fingers and closed his eyes.

"He'll sleep now. Probably go home and come back in the morning." The nurse gave her a gentle smile. "Don't worry about him. Cowboys have hard heads and this one is no different. You look like you need a sleep anyway."

"Thanks. It's been an eventful day to say the least."

"Hospital has your phone number if he needs you during the night, but you're better off getting some rest and coming back after breakfast."

"Thanks." She leaned over and kissed her husband before walking out and heading for the parking lot. There was no sign of Tyson or Libby and for that she was relieved. The drive home gave her time to reflect. She believed Chance and wondered why Libby thought her plan to waltz in and take over would work. He would have found out sooner or later if she was lying unless she planned on becoming pregnant right away, which was fine if Mother Nature was on her side.

Callie parked the truck down by the barn and saw to the animals before walking over to the holding pen where Terror was snorting his displeasure of being locked up. She crouched down and looked at his leg, deciding whether or not to call the vet or clean it up herself. It really wasn't that bad and probably wouldn't need stitching up either. A shot of antibiotics would be a good idea either way.

Using the enticement of food to lure him into a race to make her job easier, Callie shook a bucket of chaff in front of his face, happy when he lifted his nose to sniff the offering. She dumped it on the ground and climbed on the railing, the needle in her hand ready and waiting. When he dipped his head to eat, she stuck the needle into the muscle on his back and depressed the plunger, whipping back before he could react. Terror lifted his head and glared at her but continued to eat her offering.

Callie opened the race so the bull could go back into the holding yard when he was finished. That way she could keep an eye on his legs for a couple of days and then she headed for the house with Sherbet by her side.

She tossed and turned in the big bed by herself and looked at the clock between feeding times for the calf. When morning came around, Callie was ready to go and see Chance, hoping he was feeling better than he looked last night. She drove down the road toward town, glancing at Tyson's ranch as she passed. She would be ready for him today if and when he launched into a tirade against her. Now her husband was okay, there would be no holding back about her feelings for him.

The nurse smiled as Callie walked past reception and headed to Chance's room. She could hear him moaning about being in bed before she got to the door. Another nurse walked out and shook her head. "Must be better 'cause he's complaining up a storm in there. Hope you can handle him better than I can."

Callie smiled and walked to the door, peering in. "Is it safe or are you going to snap my head off, too?"

He sat propped up against the pillows, the bandage around his head holding down the messy bed hair. His face changed when he heard her voice. His color was better than it was the night before and Chance held out his arms to her. "I've been waiting for you to come in. You have to get me out of this place. I want to go home."

"Uh, don't you think you ought to wait for the doctor to tell you it's okay to leave? You had surgery, Chance." She sat on the edge of the bed and leaned into him, kissing his lips gently, wary of knocking heads with him.

Chance grabbed Callie and pulled her tight to his chest. "Didn't I tell you not to go anywhere near that bull?"

"I knew it was your fault. You can pack your bags and get the hell of the ranch." Tyson strode into the room, his face dark and thunderous.

"Tyson, wait." Chance tried to speak but his brother went over him anyway, his anger going full steam ahead.

"No. This time I'm having my say, Chance. You let her take over and look where it got you. I admit some of the people you've had on the ranch while you've been away haven't been ideal, but I've found someone who can take over starting tomorrow if we need them. I'm not letting this woman put you in danger anymore. Rory agrees, he's on his way home now."

Chance leaned forward and threw the blankets back, ready to climb out. "Now, you listen here—"

Callie held out her hand. "No, let me deal with this. I can only take so much crap before I blow my top and it's just about there now." She pressed her husband back into bed, stood up, and walked over to Tyson. Poking a finger into his chest she spoke, the diamond that had been in hiding once again gracing her hand. "For your information, pal, I will be staying on until I decide to go. You see, my husband needs me. If it wasn't for me being there, that bull would have made more of a mess than it did. Before I got there, Chance was in the paddock, undoing wire trapped around Terror's back legs, which some stupid ranch hand had left lying around. Clever, huh?" She paused for breath while noticing the color of Tyson's skin pale further.

"It was fine until he turned his back on the bull and that's when things got ugly. But not as ugly as your damned attitude toward me. I didn't ask for your opinion of my work ethics or my personality. I don't rightly care how you feel about me either, but it was your brother who asked me to marry him, not the other way around so I'm asking you to respect his choices. You don't have to like me one little bit, but kindly keep your opinion to yourself when he's around. Want to take it out on me, fine, do it later when there's just the two of us." She poked his chest once more to make her point before stepping back.

"Is she telling the truth, Chance? Did you ask her to marry you?" He stood with his hands on his hips, glancing between the two of them.

"YES, I DID. And if you have a problem with that, you can take it up with me later, not with my wife." Chance grabbed her hand and pulled her down to sit on the bed. "Give me a couple of days and I'm all yours."

Tyson scratched his head. "I don't get it. Libby said you guys were engaged and hinted that she was pregnant. What the hell's going on with that? And why would you keep your marriage a secret anyway?"

"Libby is one of the women I hung around with on the tour. It was fun while it lasted but it was nothing more than that. I doubt there's a baby and there certainly won't be a marriage. My lawyer can sort it out since she won't talk to me about it. I think it was all wishful thinking on her part." He squeezed Callie's hand. "As to why I kept my wife a secret, well. I didn't think you would believe me. I wanted you to get to know her before we told you."

"But I don't understand. You never hung around with girls like her. It was always someone famous or in the news—a model or a starlet. She's just a ranch hand."

"You really should watch how you say that. She's more than a ranch hand and worth ten of anyone like Libby. I knew you wouldn't understand if I told you I wasn't going back to the tour. I want to stay on the ranch, raise bulls, and have a life with a normal family. Callie is the normal I need."

"But you love the tour. It's what you live for." Tyson removed his hat and walked over to the window, looking out. He paused and turned back. "If you hated it so much, why did you stay away so long?"

"Initially, yes, I did love it. Plus we needed the money. The best way to get a name amongst the bull riding crowd was to be someone who won lots of cash. It all helped raise my profile and get me the rides I needed to make as much money as I could. I wanted to see you all set up for life before I quit and also I had to make sure my product line was going to sell well enough to use as backup until I started making money on breeding the bulls. Besides I figured it was the least I could do after I left you with a drunk for a father."

Tyson's mouth dropped open and Chance sighed. This wasn't going the way he wanted it to but that was the risk he was prepared to take.

"You stayed there so we could have the money you made?"

Chance nodded. No point trying to hide the fact now it was out in the open.

"I don't believe it. You didn't have to do that. We would have made it regardless, you know that."

"No, I don't. Dad never had any money, he drank it all. How do you think you'd have been able to buy the ranch if I didn't give you the money?"

"I didn't want your money. I wanted my big brother. Crappy substitution, Chance." Streaks of red lined his brother's cheeks. Anger simmered barely under the surface.

"Well, I'm sorry. I did what I thought was right at the time. I couldn't be in the same house with him. I can't change what I did back then."

Callie squeezed his hand. "I'll leave you two alone for a moment. I need coffee." She hurried away before he could stop her.

Tyson watched her leave. "You're really married to her?"

"Yes, I am. You'll like her once you get to know her." Chance smiled. "Best damned ad I ever put in a magazine, too so you can tell your friend, thanks but no thanks."

Tyson looked confused. "What? You advertised for a ranch hand or a wife?"

"Both. I got lucky when she applied." He watched the change on his brother's face. Anger to disbelief in eight seconds flat. "What's wrong with that? You've heard of dating sites. Bet you've even looked on one now and then too to see what's available." Tyson looked away but not before Chance saw the confirmation in his eyes. "Ha, got you."

"So what? I've looked but that doesn't mean I've put my name down or anything. That's just weird. Like having a mail order bride." He leaned his denim clad butt against the window sill. "So, what happens when you go back on the tour, she staying home?"

"Told you already, I want to stay here and raise bulls and a family."

"I don't believe you."

"Well, get used to the idea, Tyson. I couldn't go back even if I wanted to, not with my hip like it is. Doctors tell me it'll never be like it was. I can live with that. Just so happens it came at the right time for me. I've been unhappy with it for a couple of years now. Probably the reason Terror got one up on me; my mind wasn't focused on the job." He smoothed down the blanket covering his knees. "I'm hoping Callie will want to stay."

Tyson eased down on the edge of the bed. "What do you mean, hope she'll stay? I thought you married her and you're talking about a family."

"I did. But as far as she's concerned, it was only a twelve-month contract. Told her I wanted a divorce at the end of it because by then I figured the Libby's of the world would have forgotten about me and I'd get a peaceful life."

"And she agreed?"

"Yeah. Poor thing lost her parents in a car crash, leaving behind a spread so far into debt it wasn't funny. Apparently they've been locked in a drought for years with no hope of things getting better, they had to borrow to feed the cattle." He wiped his hand over his chin, wondering if he had any chance of making his brothers understand his actions. He was starting to doubt himself. "The bank took the farm and Callie was left with a huge debt. I made her a down payment as part of the contract with the promise of another one after the stipulated period."

"But I thought you wanted to stay married to her?"

"I do. That's the problem. She thinks she's going home and I'm not sure I can convince her to stay."

Chapter Eighteen

CHANCE LOOKED UP when there was a tap on the door. Callie stood there with Rory by her side. "Look who I found. You guys look so alike I figured it had to be a relative. Thought you might like to have another visitor."

"Rory." His brother walked in and gave him a restrained hug before moving over to Tyson, slapping him on the back before standing next to him. Callie walked in and sat on the edge of the bed and took Chance's hand again.

"The things you'll do to get attention." Rory grinned looking cheerful, but Chance could see the sadness that still haunted his brother in his eyes.

"Yeah, well, got you all here so I suppose it worked." He lifted Callie's hand to his mouth and kissed it. "You've met my beautiful bride."

"Yes, outside, but I didn't know you guys were married. Best you fill me in then."

Chance repeated the story he'd told Tyson but leaving out the bit about trying to convince Callie to stay.

"Pleased for you, brother. Congratulations to you both."

He came over and kissed Callie on the cheek before shaking his brother's hand. "I hope you'll be very happy together."

"Thanks, I appreciate it. So, have you got the job?" Chance noted the shadow in Callie's eyes and started planning on how and when to tell her he didn't want to let her go.

Rory nodded his head. "Yep, came through right after I spoke to you. I was going to drive up next week, but Tyson called me late last night so I jumped in my truck and here I am."

Tyson slapped him on the shoulder. "Thanks for telling me you were moving back home."

"Why would I? You can't keep a damned secret. Last thing I wanted was you telling the whole town. I like to make my own announcements, thanks."

Tyson grunted and then a look of delight came into his eyes. "Talking of secrets. Guess you didn't know what else big brother has been holding out on us?" Without waiting for an answer, he kept talking. "Seems our little sister-in-law here is the town of Marietta's first mail order bride."

"What? How come?"

Chance went through the story again and also filled him in on the reason he wouldn't be going back to the rodeo as well.

"Mail order bride. Well, I never would have believed it." Rory rubbed his hand over his chin, looking at Chance with a spark of interest in his eyes.

"Worked for me, could easily work for you guys, too, you know."

"Nah, don't even go there." Tyson was adamant in his protest.

"Is there something you aren't telling us, little brother?" Rory winked at Chance. "About time you showed some interest in something other than your horses."

"I'm quite happy as I am. Don't go making anything out of it either. Not like I have the time or the money for courting anyone. Trying my hardest to build up the business."

"I'm sure the right woman would be more than happy to help you do that, Tyson." Callie smiled encouragingly at him and Chance watched as his brother blushed.

"How about you, Rory? Ever give any thoughts to trying again?" Chance held his breath.

"Maybe, maybe not. Depends on the day. Let's leave that one for now and concentrate on getting you out of here shall we? When are they letting you go home?"

Chance squeezed his wife's hand. "Tomorrow if all goes well. I feel much better and the doctor is happy with progress. Luckily, my darling wife is such a hard ass. If she hadn't come along when she did and pushed Terror away, I'd be a mess right about now."

He saw the sheen of tears in Callie's eyes.

"It's true. I've put myself in harm's way for far too long. I need to be more careful in future and with you by my side, I think I can do that. We have so much to look forward to."

CALLIE SWALLOWED THE emotions threatening to choke her as she listened to Chance talk about their future. Yesterday, she wasn't even sure they had one together now she was hoping for a miracle. She hoped what he was saying wasn't for the benefit of his brothers alone. The fear clutching at her heart when she saw Terror attacking Chance was nothing she had felt before and it scared the crap out of her.

"Well, maybe next time you'll think a little before you do something so damned stupid. I'd hate to have to pick up after you all the time."

"Is it an Aussie thing, the way she talks to you?" Rory grinned as he asked the question.

"Yeah, I think so. It's just how she rolls, telling it like it is." Chance lifted her hand to his lips and kissed her palm. If the brothers weren't in the same room, she would have locked the door and had her way with him right there and then. One day without him in her bed and she was getting antsy already.

"I'd better go and let you have some time with these guys. I'll be back later today. Don't give the nurses a hard time, you hear?"

"Don't go on our account, Callie." Tyson walked over and stood beside her. "Um, I may as well get this over and done with." He rubbed his hand around the back of his neck and cleared his throat. "It's just that I think I owe you an apology."

"Yeah, you're right. You do." She stood up and faced him, hands tucked into the back pockets of her jeans.

He looked to the hospital bed for help but all Chance did was shrug his shoulders.

"Right, then. Okay." He took a deep breath. "I was out of line. You deserved more respect than I gave you and for that I'm sorry."

"And?" Callie tilted her head and waited.

"And, um, well…" He looked at Rory for help but the deputy just shook his head. "I don't know what more you want."

"Really? Well let me tell you then so you don't make the same mistake again. How about you learn to respect your brother's decisions and you promise you won't butt in again if it's something that doesn't concern you. That'd be good for a start, I reckon."

Tyson pursed his lips. "Fine. I promise to respect my brother's decisions and not butt into things that don't concern me."

Callie slapped him on the shoulder. "Great start. Thanks, apology accepted." She turned away, leaned down and kissed her husband. "Be good and I'll be back soon, okay?" Callie looked to Rory. "How about I make up the guest room and you can come and stay with us for a few days until you figure out what you want to do and where you want to live. I could sure do with the company."

"Are you sure it's not inconvenient?"

"Not at all. We'd love to have you stay." She looked at her husband.

"What she said." Chance laughed. "Truly, Rory, we have plenty of room."

Tyson looked offended and piped up. "So do I. He can stay with me, too."

"Sorry, Tyson. I don't think I could handle living with you right now. Hell, I still remember how nosy you were when we were kids. Doubt you've changed that much."

"I'm not nosy. Just have a curious nature is all." He crossed his arms and huffed as they laughed at him.

"Yeah, well, I'd rather you weren't curious on my part for now." He turned to Callie. "If you're sure it's alright, that'd be great. I can drive on up later after I've had a look around town and called in at the office to do a meet and greet."

"Wonderful. Well, then, I'll see you all later." Callie waved her fingers as she left the Watson boys alone.

Chapter Nineteen

CALLIE HELPED CHANCE out of the truck and onto the porch. "I'm okay. Not even the slightest bit dizzy. Just a few bruises that are looking pretty colorful right now." He eased down onto a chair and gazed over the valley.

"Let me get a couple of mugs of coffee and we can relax out here for a bit while the weather is nice." Callie headed inside and Chance dropped his hand to Sherbet's head. The dog had been sitting at the door waiting for them when they got home and she sidled up to his chair. "Guess I owe you, don't I, girl? Heard tell you got in between me and Terror." He stroked her ears and smiled as she leaned into him. "Got lucky big time, the pair of us didn't we?"

Callie came back out and placed the cups on the table between chairs.

"Sit with me." Chance patted the edge of his chair and she perched down beside him. "Best decision I ever made bringing you here. You know that, don't you?" He cupped her chin and turned her to face him. Her smile was beautiful to see and he'd kicked himself when he remembered her scream when Terror attacked. He never wanted to put her through anything like that again.

"Yep. Couldn't have said it better myself. I'm glad Tyson has come around."

"Me, too. I'm sorry I had to keep you a secret from him. It wasn't the cleverest way to go about it."

"No, probably not, but it all worked out for the best. I'm glad Rory has come home for your sake. He seems a really nice guy."

"He is. One of the most down to earth and calm guys I know. He'll be good for the town. I just hope he finds someone as nice as you. He deserves another chance at love."

"Yes, he does. He spoke about his wife last night. I felt so sad for him, too. Finding out you're going to be a parent and losing everything in the space of a day must have been gut-wrenching for him. I'm not sure I understand how he made it through that."

"Strong man. I just wish Evan would come home, too. I miss him."

"Well now, it will give you something to work on while you recover. Get in touch and convince him to come home and settle down. You did it, now you can work on Evan." Callie picked up her coffee and took a sip, watching the cogs turn over in his brain.

"You don't mean what I think you mean, do you?" Chance grinned.

"What are you talking about?"

"Find them brides of their own?" He leaned over for a quick kiss. "I like how your mind works, wife."

"Stands to reason, doesn't it? If you're happy and settled, they'd want to come back to town and live here. As to the wives part, I don't know them so I can only talk in general terms. What man wouldn't like to come back to a wife and happy home every evening?"

Chance picked up his coffee and Callie touched mugs with him, the possibilities already going through her mind.

"I'LL LEAVE THAT with you then while I go and do my chores. Don't want to see you move out of that chair until I get back, understood?" Callie stood up. "I won't be long, promise."

"I don't have any intention of moving. Sitting here looking down at the valley is the perfect way for me to spend the next couple of hours." Chance lifted his lips for a kiss. She obliged and sauntered off down to the barn to feed the calf and look over the rest of the stock. Once the cows had been checked, along with making sure the calves were all feeding, she glanced over at the bull who'd tried to kill her husband.

Terror's leg looked much better with no signs of infection so she let him out of the holding yard. He stamped his feet, trying to intimidate her. She laughed from her position up on the railing of the crusher. "Don't scare me, old boy.

Just remember, if you don't perform with those pretty little girls, you'll be steak before you know it. After that last little episode, it won't take much for me to send you to the butchers."

She watched him walk away and head butt some of the younger bulls, taking out his annoyance at being locked up on them before he put his head down and started to feast on the green grass. "Come on, Sherbet. Let's get out of here while he's busy." Callie hurried out of the paddock. With her hands tucked into her jeans pockets to keep warm, she sauntered back toward the house.

A black town car sat parked next to the truck and she wondered who owned it. An elegant lady sat on the chair next to Chance and stood when Callie walked up onto the porch. She held out her hand. "You must be Callie. I've heard so much about you."

Callie looked at Chance, a question in the air between them. "Callie, this is Jane Weiss, Director for the Marietta Chamber of Commerce."

"Hi. Nice to meet you." Callie perched on the side of Chance's chair and reached for his hand.

"Jane has heard a little rumor that I'm not going back to the tour and wanted to discuss this year's upcoming Marietta Rodeo with me."

Jane sat forward, her face glowing with excitement. "Yes. I'm sorry that you had to retire, Chance, but if you'd just hear me out." She looked at Callie. "Your husband was one of the best bull riders in history as I'm sure you know. The chamber has had a meeting and we want Chance to be the honorary chair for the next rodeo. It will bring in so many people to town if they know he's there and I'm beyond excited to see what it will do for the local businesses."

"Honorary chair?" Callie glanced at her husband. "What's that?"

Jane laughed and sat back, letting Chance do the explaining.

"DRAW CARD I guess is the easiest way to explain it." He grinned. "Since I have such a great fan base, it makes sense some of them will come to the rodeo, if only to meet me and catch up. Bring business to the town, too, which we'd never turn down."

"Actually, it's more than that. Chance is selling himself short as always. The honorary chair is the position given to someone who has made a great impact on the IBR and rodeo business. Your husband has been such a beacon of light in all the years he's been involved in the sport. And having a great fan base is slightly downplaying things. He has an incredible fan base. People follow him all over the country. But, apart from that, he's a decent man that promoted the tour, encouraged more young people to join, and had a hand in raising money for needy charities along the way. And that was in his own time, too. Most of it outside the rodeo season."

Callie turned her head and looked at him. "Really? So much more than just a bull rider then. You never told me all that. I'm proud of you, Chance."

"You should be, Callie. He's an amazing man. So what do you think, Chance? Can I tell the team you'll be the one?"

"I guess that'll be fine. What do you say. Callie. Want to ride the lead float with me at the parade and dance with me on the Saturday night?"

"I like the sound of that." She turned back to Jane. "We had rodeos at home in Australia but I doubt they'd be anything as big as what you're used to. I can't wait to see it."

"Fall will roll around before you know it. Now the hard work really begins. We have a lot of planning to do. I'd best get back to town and spread the good news."

Chance put his hand up. "Look, Jane, I haven't announced my retirement yet. Think you can hold off for a week or so? I don't mind you telling the committee but not the general public yet." He gritted his teeth. "My family know now and I promised my manager he could say something after that."

She stood up. "Of course, Chance. As soon as I see something in the news about it I'll put the announcement on our website, how's that?"

"Fine by me. Thanks for understanding, Jane." He made

to stand up to see her off but she put a motherly hand on his shoulder.

"Stay there with your lovely wife. I can see myself to the car." She waved her fingers and turned away from them.

Chance and Callie watched the tail lights disappear down the driveway.

"Honorary chair, eh? Sounds like fun." She frowned and looked away over the valley.

"Yeah, I guess, but I'm sensing you're not convinced. Tell me what's wrong, Callie."

"I won't be here. I'm not complaining mind. It's been fun working for you and being your temporary wife but I'll be back in Australia by then."

"What if I don't want you to go?"

She turned to look at him, a sheen of tears in her eyes.

"I mean it, Callie. I fell in love with you the day I met you. I knew you were what I wanted in a wife, a life partner. I don't want you to go home."

"Seriously?"

He grinned. "Yeah."

She stood up, took a few steps away from him. Callie looked over the valley with her hands stuck in her pants pockets. Her silence scared him. If she didn't say something soon, he would start to panic.

"Why?" She glanced over her shoulder at him. "I know you had reasons for doing this how you did but you never really told me why."

He sat up, beckoned her to sit with him.

With his arms around her, Chance spoke. "My mother died when I was ten as you already know. For me, family life all but ended then, too. Our father turned to the bottle and there were no more hugs goodnight, no kisses when we scraped our knees." He leaned his chin on her shoulder. "When I won my first competition, I fell in love for the first time. At least it was love on my side. She was only after the fame and took off to be with the next guy as soon as he was king of the hill."

Chance laughed, remembering how naive he'd been. "After the same thing happened a few times, I figured either I was unlovable or they were only after fame and fortune. Seems the latter was true because when Libby got her hooks into me she made it plain as day that we'd be good for each other. My money would get her the movies that she wanted. Sadly for her, I didn't fall for it. I'd wised up by then."

"I'm not surprised. But you were starved for love, Chance. I understand it."

"Yeah, well, it seems I was kind of slow figuring it out but once I had, I decided that if I married you it would take me out of the public eye and sooner or later the money chasing women would forget me. I could get a divorce and live a quiet life up here, maybe meet a nice ranching girl who didn't know me from a bar of soap."

"But you've changed your mind?"

"Yes, I have. I know you don't care about my money.

You've proved that already and you're nothing like the other women in my life. How long do you think someone like Libby would last up here? She couldn't stand to get her hands dirty where as you're keen to get in and get things done. That's the kind of woman I want to spend my days with, rear a family with."

Callie turned, dropped a kiss on his lips and snuggled in closer to him. "I don't know how I would have left you either. I feel so at home here with you."

"So you'll stay? Promise?"

"Yes, I promise. I'm not going anywhere, cowboy. Not now you've told me you love me."

Epilogue

CALLIE CLAPPED WILDLY as Chance did a round of the floor with Miss Marietta Rodeo Teen in his arms. Dressed to kill in his best outfit, he'd made the lively fourteen-year-old Maggie Thompson blush as he spun her around the room while the whole town watched and wolf-whistled.

"Having fun?" Rory pushed his way in beside her to watch his elder brother do his honorary chair duties.

"Heck, yes. This is awesome. I've been to some big local rodeos but this is something else." She took the glass of punch he held out to her. The cold drink slid down her parched throat and Callie sighed. "I'm so glad he took Jane up on her offer. This has been the best weekend and I think it's been great for the town."

"Sure has. Place is fit to bust with visitors." Rory tapped his foot to the music. "You don't think he misses it, do you? Being in the thick of competition?"

"I don't think so. His accident came at the right time according to him. He's happy now. Gets to work on the ranch full-time and lay his head down in the same bed every night."

Rory laughed and Callie nudged him in the ribs.

"Don't even go there. We're very happy, Rory. I want him to stay that way." She turned back to the dancers.

Chance gave Maggie a final spin as the music came to a halt and then walked her back to her parents. He spoke a few words and looked over to Callie, winked and tipped his hat at Maggie. Then he turned and walked back across the dance floor to his wife.

"I've been saving this dance for you." Ignoring the smirk on his brothers face, Chance held out his hand to his wife and waited for her to take it.

Callie swallowed, poked her tongue between her lips and sighed when she heard the tune start up. "You are such a hopeless romantic. I love it." She placed her hand in his and he pulled her out onto the dance floor letting his other hand slide down her back and rest just above her butt. A small press of his fingers let her know how hard it was to be circumspect in public. She grinned and a blush rose on her cheeks.

"You have a major fan after that dance, cowboy."

He twirled her around and made his way into the center of the room. "I know. Great kid, she'll make a great ambassador for Marietta's youngsters."

Callie rested her cheek against his neck as they danced the slow waltz together. Her words were quiet but loud enough for him to hear. "Are you really happy, Chance? Not being part of the bull-riding scene anymore?"

He pressed his lips onto her temple. "I've never missed it, not one bit. I thought you knew that."

"I did. But with you being involved like this I wondered if it would bring back memories for you. Make you miss it all and wish you were back there."

He leaned back so he could look into her face. The freckles on her nose stood out under the bright lights. "I have everything I want and more. The day I met you at the alter was the day my new life started. It's all I've ever wanted."

"Are you sure?"

"Well, there is one thing I want more." He paused, slid his hand down over her butt and pulled her against him.

"What?"

"Let's get out of here where we can be alone and I'll show you."

THE END

Ready for the rodeo?

The 78th Copper Mountain Rodeo series

Catch Me, Cowboy by Jeannie Watt

Protect Me, Cowboy by Shelli Stevens

Want Me, Cowboy by Sinclair Jayne

Love Me, Cowgirl by Eve Gaddy

Available now at your favorite online retailer!

About the Author

After moving to the lush green wine region of Australia's Hunter Valley, Ann has the perfect surrounding to let her imagination to run wild. She alternates her time between writing western romances, women's fiction romantic and playing in her garden.

Two kinds of hero make Ann to a mass of nerves. The hot cowboy with a slow sexy drawl (she used to live out in the desert and enjoyed every minute) and a man in a kilt. (Imagine Jamie Fraser) She can't wait to visit Scotland where she can get her fill of the tartan clad hotties for, um research purposes, of course.

In the meantime, her dear husband puts up with her talking to her characters and getting lost in worlds only she can imagine as she battles to bring stories to the page for everyone to enjoy.

Visit her website at AnnBHarrisonRomance.com

Thank you for reading

Chance for Love

If you enjoyed this book, you can find more from all our great authors at TulePublishing.com, or from your favorite online retailer.

TULE
PUBLISHING

21795720R00127

Printed in Poland
by Amazon Fulfillment
Poland Sp. z o.o., Wrocław